Coyote Peterson's
Brave Adventures

Wild Animals in a Wild World

Cover Illustration - Patrick Brickman
Field Journal Illustrations - Dia Windhoffer
Narrative Story Illustrations - Margret M. Krister
Layout Design: Elina Diaz

For permission requests, please contact the publisher at:

Mango Publishing Group
2850 Douglas Road, 3rd Floor
Coral Gables, FL 33134 USA
info@mango.bz

For special orders, quantity sales, course adoptions and corporate sales, please email the publisher at sales@mango.bz. For trade and wholesale sales, please contact Ingram Publisher Services at customer.service@ingramcontent.com or +1.800.509.4887.

Coyote Peterson's Brave Adventures : Wild Animals in a Wild World

Library of Congress Cataloging
ISBN: (paperback) 978-1-63353-943-3, (hardcover) 978-1-63353-577-0, (ebook) 978-1-63353-578-7
Library of Congress Control Number: 2017947631
BISAC category code : JNF002000 JUVENILE NONFICTION / Adventure & Adventurers

Printed in the United States of America

"The things we fear in life often lead to our greatest adventures."

– Coyote Peterson

This book is dedicated to the Coyote Pack; without each and every one of you, these Brave Adventures would not be possible. To my crew for their fearless ability to break trail into the wild where they somehow follow me with cameras. To my incredible family for their never-ending belief that impossible dreams can come true.

"Creating wildlife segments with Coyote Peterson and the crew has given me the chance to get up close with some of the most amazing animals on earth while experiencing the reality of my childhood dreams... to become a wildlife professional spreading awareness and passion to the next generation. For that I am grateful."

– Mario Aldecoa
Brave Wilderness Wildlife Producer

"Coyote's idea of vacation is camping on an ...extremely-snake infested island... in the middle of Lake Erie, catching snakes and seeing which bite him... for science of course. I've been witnessing him do this for over a decade now. What more can I say?"

– Chris Kost
Brave Wilderness Editor

"Never in my wildest dreams did I ever think I would have some of the life experiences and animal encounters that I have had working with Coyote. His ambition and contagious enthusiasm pushes all of us to some truly amazing places... now it's your turn!"

– **Chance Ross**
Brave Wilderness Videographer

"Adventure changes you – needless to say following Coyote Peterson with my camera has changed me. Together we have journeyed through scorching deserts, perilous swamps and forests so dense each step requires the swing of a machete... yet with each step I always find myself more inspired than the one before it. That's why true adventure never ends."

– **Mark Laivins**
Director of Brave Wilderness

Contents

Prologue

To the Parents...

My name is Coyote Peterson, and for as long as I can remember I have been absolutely fascinated with animals. As a child, I spent a great deal of my time exploring the woods behind the house where I grew up in the small town of Newbury, Ohio, and it was those experiences that provided me with the perfect backdrop to develop my sense of love and passion for adventure. Every day, from sunup to sundown, I was on the search for frogs, snakes, turtles and pretty much any other creature that I could observe or hopefully catch.

These early adventures of mucking around in swamps and ponds led me down an inspiring path of amazement and curiosity about the natural world. Every week my mom would take me to the public library where I could scour countless books to help me unlock the mysteries of these incredible animals I was finding, and from there, my thirst for knowledge about wildlife became insatiable. I would check one book out, read it, return it, and get another one! To me, books were fantastic and enlightening; they became my imagination's guide to the great outdoors and everything that the world had to offer.

However, I will never forget discovering animal adventure shows on television. I couldn't believe it... these people were doing the same thing I was doing in my own backyard, but they were traveling all over the world! Instead of catching frogs and turtles, they were catching crocodiles, anacondas, and even swimming with great white sharks!

My young mind absorbed every piece of content it could possibly find, from reruns of Mutual of Omaha's *Wild Kingdom* to the late great Steve Irwin's *Crocodile Hunter*; if it had animals and adventure, I was glued to it. Although I loved watching and learning about all the animals, I was becoming equally fascinated with the hosts of these great TV shows. I marveled at how they could capture these amazing encounters on camera and project them directly to my television.

It was in these moments that I had the realization that this was exactly what I wanted to do with my life. I wanted to be the guy who was catching the animals, talking to the camera, and educating the audience. From those early days, I told my Mom that I wanted to have my own reptile show some day. I wanted to be the one to show other people this incredible world that I had come to love and respect. She smiled and told me, "You can do anything you want... never give up on your dreams."

So, as I moved onto high school and then college, I began studying the art of filmmaking, particularly from the writing, directing, and producing standpoint. I knew that if I ever wanted to become a host in front of the camera that I first had to understand how the shows were made from behind the camera. I watched my favorite series over and over, studying the scripts, shots, and directing style. I convinced my friends to start producing with me and we began writing our own scripts, which soon led to filming our own test pilots, which we amusingly called "sizzle reels." For years, we developed our skill sets and honed what we felt was great animal adventure entertainment. Then, when the time was absolutely right, we launched our YouTube channel and *Brave Wilderness* was born.

Breaking Trail, Dragon Tails, Beyond the Tide, Coyote's Backyard, and *On Location*: these shows became the backbone of the Brave Wilderness channel. As I sit here preparing to write my first book chronicling some of my bravest adventures to date, I feel incredibly fortunate to have been given the chance to live this journey.

People often ask, "How did you became an animal adventure show host?" The truth is, I did it by combining the inspiration that I gained from my predecessors, a self-taught knowledge of wildlife, and my formal education in filmmaking. Plus some incredible friends and family, a whole lot of trial and error, countless bites, bumps, bruises and the unrelenting belief that I could actually make a living pursuing my own imagination! I truly am a living embodiment of the old saying "If you can dream it, you can do it." It is this belief in one's self that I hope to pass on to anyone who takes an interest in my story.

To the Coyote Pack...

I have said it before, and I'll say it again. The Brave Wilderness team and I could not do this without you; the reader, the viewer... the member of the pack. You know who you are, and believe me when I say you are an incredibly important part of this team and this journey. It's an expedition that we are all on together, and right now I am honored and humbled to be the one who is leading the adventure. But you never know, one day it might be you who is writing a book just like this, born from the inspiration you found in our work, as we continue to bring animal education and entertainment to the world through Brave Wilderness.

Thank you for reading, you have my promise that every chapter is going to be an action-packed animal adventure!

Be Brave, Stay Wild!
Coyote

Chapter 1

The Dragon

A ll great stories start at the beginning, and in this case our beginning happens to be on a warm summer evening when I was eight years old. They call this time of day "golden hour" because as the sun cascades through the tree branches, it breaks apart into warm light, illuminating the meadow grasses and causing the landscape to radiate a beautiful golden hue. Golden hour is the perfect time of day to encounter animals.

As I yanked on my rubber muck boots and cut through the glowing grasses, my stride was fixed on quickly making it down to the lake. Welcome to my backyard. Now keep in mind, my backyard was no ordinary backyard with a mowed lawn, a picket fence, and a sand box. My backyard was an epic expanse of untamed wilderness composed of endless forests, rolling meadows, winding creeks, and one enormous lake at the center of it all.

Crickets orchestrated my soundtrack, and as I drew closer to the water's edge, the echoing sound of the evening's first bullfrogs croaked out with an unmistakable deep bellow, a surefire sign that the wetland ecosystem was alive with activity. Water snakes skittered along the embankments searching for prey, muskrats breached the surface of the water dancing in the flickering light, and a great blue heron stealthily stalked for fish in the shallows. I stopped at the edge of the lake as my boots squished into the primordial mud and I closed my eyes. I felt a moment of peace as I connected with the wild and whispered to myself.

"Let today... be the day... that I am brave enough to face The Dragon."

The Dragon. As an eight-year-old boy, nothing captures your imagination more than believing that dragons DO EXIST and that you have the bravery deep down inside to actually capture one. Capture a dragon? Wait a minute. Capture... a DRAGON? Yes, you heard me right.

Follow me for a moment – close your eyes, and as you leave your human body to become one with nature, pretend that you are a fish or a frog. Now dive beneath the water's surface and into the aquatic world of this giant lake. You are swimming under the weed beds and dodging around lily pad stems through a complicated maze of unknown wonders. Then, all of a sudden you round an old rotting log on the basin of the lake and WHAM! In a flash of power your world blooms white – and before you even know what has happened, you have been eaten by a Snapping Turtle!

Now open your eyes. Phew! Good thing you are still human!

These reptiles, the Common Snapping Turtles, are armed with a massive bone-crushing beak and razor-sharp claws, defended with a gnarled algae-covered shell and a long, spiked tail, and

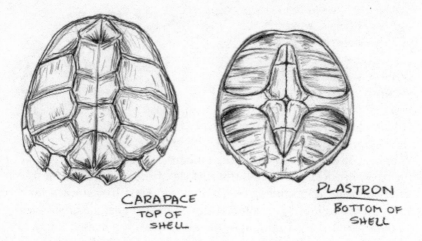

CARAPACE
TOP OF
SHELL

PLASTRON
BOTTOM OF
SHELL

prehistorically painted with camouflage that makes them almost invisible to the untrained eye. They are without question the last true dragons that call our wetlands home, and today I was going to capture one... the biggest one in this lake... or at least that is what I told myself as I snapped back into reality and realized that my boots had sunk nearly knee-deep in the mud!

"Dang! Stuck again!"

I toppled backwards butt-first and landed on the embankment, and after pulling with all my might, I finally freed my feet enough to stand up. Clunky start, but I dusted myself off and slowly began to creep along the edge of the lake.

Shadows and stealth are what make the snapping turtle so lethal. You see, if you're a member of an unsuspecting prey species and you are being hunted by a predator who knows how to use the shadows to its advantage... there is a good chance you will become a meal. How does that work, you ask? Well, most prey species feed under the illumination of light, while the shadows keep the predators hidden, allowing them to stalk up stealthily below their prey while staying completely unnoticed. Then as soon as the unsuspecting target gets close to the edge, where the shadows meet the light... SNAAAAP! Dinner is served.

In this scenario, I considered myself the predator and the snapping turtle my prey. Trust me when I say that only an eight-year-old Coyote would have such a thought. Looking back at this experience now, I am pretty sure I was nowhere near predator status in these early adventures. However, my goal was to use the golden hour to my advantage when it came to sneaking up on this turtle. In the early evenings snapping turtles move from the deep into shallower waters to hunt along the lake's edge. I knew that if I found myself in the right place at the right time, I might stand a chance of making a miraculous catch.

How did I know this, you may be asking? Well, I had been down this road several times before. I would spot the giant turtle near the lake's edge and take a step into the water toward it, the turtle would notice me... and then WHOOSH! In a flurry of webbed feet and disturbed mud, it would disappear into the shadowy depths, and I would be left there contemplating what I did wrong. My stealth tactics were accurate, but what I lacked was the cover of shadows. From beneath the surface, I am certain that the turtle saw a giant towering figure and said to itself, "Oh boy, that looks like trouble! I'm outta here!" This is the scenario that had played out numerous times over the course of this particular summer... but little did I know, today was going to be different.

The sunlight was getting to be the perfect angle; just enough light breaching the surface to illuminate the basin of the lake's edges, where I could see tadpoles and small fish dancing as I stalked along the sides. I was making my way to the far corner of the lake, a treacherous zone of deep, body-swallowing mud that was topped with tangling pond weeds and a perfect layer of clear water on top; an ideal hunting zone for snapping turtles.

This particular body of water was actually home to several snapping turtles. I knew this because to date I had captured five of them, all of which were average sized, weighing around twenty pounds. Then there was the big one, the one

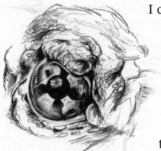

I called Dragon – little did I know that as I was slowly rounding the embankment, I was entering his lair.

Snapping Turtles are territorial, and once a large male has found a plentiful food supply it will guard this area aggressively against encroaching turtles. The Dragon was enormous, and I am willing to bet that no turtle in the lake would ever dare challenge his territorial throne. Good thing for me is that I was not a turtle, although now that I think about it... maybe it would have been wiser not to challenge this mammoth reptile.

My eyes were razor sharp with precision as I scanned the surface of the water looking for a trail of bubbles... a sure sign that a turtle was moving beneath the surface. Nothing. I stood and waited with the warm summer breeze dancing off the ends of my T-shirt; my fingertips twisted the tops of the long grasses as I studied the water with anticipation, the sun barely escaping through the tree branches. I was losing light quickly and so far there was no sign of this ancient creature. I began to walk further around the edge of the lake, when suddenly a small group of bluegill fish darted from beneath the pond weeds and scattered in an incredible panic into deeper water. I stopped dead in my tracks, knowing that one thing and one thing alone can scare a group of fish like that: a snapping turtle.

The bed of weeds was dense, spanning about 15 feet in length, and on my end I couldn't see a thing. No bubbles, no movement... no visible sign of the turtle. I decided to move a little further ahead and position myself at the far end of the weed bed. If the fish were coming toward me, that meant whatever scared them was also coming in my direction. I was moving as quietly as I could, but my boots sank into the mud and made a suctioning sound with every step I took. It was hard to focus on the water when I was in a constant battle to simply keep my boots on my feet. Each and every step was a muddy challenge until I came to the front end of the weed bed and squinted my eyes into the setting sun.

With the light reflecting off the water, I tilted my head left and right, desperately trying to focus my gaze through the glare on the surface. Something was there. An obscure shape, like a floating rock, right up against the weed bed. As my eyes slowly adjusted I realized that the obscure shape before me was a massive, foot-long tail decorated with algae and covered in spikes that just happened to run straight into the back end of an enormous snapping turtle! THE snapping turtle. This... was... THE DRAGON!

There are moments in your life where time becomes divided into two parts... "before this" and "after this." I was stuck in a state of limbo, partially because my boots were sinking in mud, but also because my body was paralyzed with fear and excitement. Little did I know that these coming moments would change the direction of my life FOREVER.

With the Dragon less than two feet away from me and his front half tucked under the weed bed, I could definitely see him, but he could not see me. My mind began to race with strategy and anticipation.

"What do I do? What do I do?!?"

I had my shot at catching this turtle – and he was huge... strike that, I mean MASSIVE! As an eight-year-old, I probably stood on the bathroom scale and pushed the needle to about sixty-five pounds, and this turtle would easily top out right around fifty! This was one giant reptile!

By now the sounds of nature had fallen silent; the frogs, the crickets, the wind... everything was still. I carefully and quietly lifted my left leg, my boot sucking at the mud with a gulping sound as it released. I stood on one foot... the turtle had not moved. Holding my breath, I gently stepped deeper into the water, trying not to disturb the environment in any way whatsoever. With the toe of my boot cutting through the water's surface, my leg submerged and went down deep; well over the rim of my boot. Almost instantly the water flooded in, soaking my foot, and a tar-like ooze soon followed, turning my sock black.

"Oh boy, Mom is gonna make me
throw out this pair of socks for sure...
but who cares! This is the Dragon... this
is my moment!"

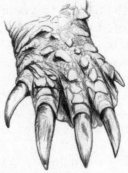

I was now less than a foot from the
reptile – it was within arm's reach.
I could feel beads of sweat running
down my face as the hairs on the back
of my neck stood up. My heart was in
maximum overdrive, and its beats echoed in
my eardrums. I began to lean down toward the
water, and then... the turtle moved! Not a lot, just a little, but it
was very slowly beginning to turn. The reptile was hunting, and I
prayed that I had not just become its target.

The back edge of its shell, which was sculpted with jagged spikes,
continued to turn towards me. I needed to act quickly. If it turned
all the way, my opportunity would be lost, because I had to catch
it from the back of its shell, otherwise I would be looking straight
into the face of the beast and those bone-crushing jaws.

'Do it Coyote... grab the back of the turtle's shell before it turns
around and you lose your shot at landing The Dragon. Do it, Do
it, Do...'

Then in a blind moment of insanity, I plunged
my arms into the water and grabbed onto
the back of its shell!

The world stood still; not a sound,
not a gust of wind, just a complete
empty silence in my mind. In that
moment, the silence lasted for
hours; but in reality, it lasted for
less than a second – and then BOOOOOM!
My world exploded! In a fury of claws and
splashing, the giant reptile realized
something, or in this case someone, had
grabbed it. The massive upper shell, which

was covered in green slimy algae, breached the surface and sent a tidal wave of water crashing over my arms and soaking my clothes.

A sharp piercing pain suddenly shot up my arm, just after my mind realized that I had taken a handful of razor-sharp claws. I let go of the turtle and fell backward.

The Dragon spun in confusion as my mind spun in a daze.

"My hands... are off the turtle!" It was getting away! "NOOOOOO!!!" I screamed as I rocketed to my feet.

With my boots stuck in the mud, I pulled my feet free from them and went headfirst into the water after the turtle. In a blind grab of faith, I managed to latch back onto the turtle's shell, and boy, was it angry! Fifty pounds of ferocious reptile began to pull me out into the deeper water. I was nearly waist deep and panic was beginning to set in.

"What if this turtle drags me under... what if it turns around and bites me... what if it EATS ME?"

I can tell you this much, snapping turtles don't eat humans.

But at eight years old, anything is possible in your imagination! I held on with all my might, my hands fighting to keep their grasp on its slippery algae-covered shell. The creature's clawed feet fought against me, sending waves of water into my face while its massive head twisted and reared around as it relentlessly tried to bite me. The battle was on, and I dug my sock-covered feet into the mud... I had reached the point of no return!

Just another couple steps forward and I was going to be in over my head – but a couple steps backward and I would have a chance of dragging this ancient looking beast up and out of the ooze. With teeth clenched, I pulled with all my might, slipping in the mud and water. Finally, I gained my footing, and in that instant the turtle's head rose to the surface, its jaws open wide. The beast turned and looked right at me with its golden diamond eyes, the most beautiful yet terrifying thing I had ever seen, as it hissed something awful. The smell of death plumed from its gut, the remains of countless fish and frogs reaching my nostrils and sending my head back with a jolt. It might as well have been a fireball from the belly of a mythological dragon. It was so disarming that I nearly lost my grip.

This was the moment I had been dreaming of, face-to-face with a real life, modern-day DRAGON! I refused to let go.

'PULL COYOTE... PUUUULLLLL!'

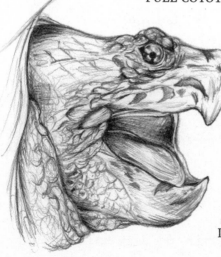

I took a step back, and the turtle lunged, causing me to slip and collapse onto a single knee.

'DON'T LET GO!'

I stood back up... and pulled again, one more step toward the shore. Sweat mixed with mud ran down my forehead and into my eyes. I shut the left one and winced

in pain at the fiery sting.
My mind screamed, "Sweat and mud will not defeat me today!"

Another strong pull and another few inches gained. This was a literal tug-of-war against one of the most powerful reptiles in the world, and somehow I was winning! My toes dug into the mud through my socks, and I put every ounce of strength I had into another pull... the turtle's shell was now completely visible, its massive prehistoric tail covered in mud and glistening in the setting sunlight.

I could not believe it – there it was right before my very eyes.

"The Dragon is Real!"

After a final pull, I could feel my feet on solid ground, the turtle still clutched in my hands as its dagger-like claws sliced through the mud, attempting an escape. One more step back and the meadow grasses began pricking at my legs. Then, by some miracle of eight-year-old strength, I heaved the giant turtle up and onto the embankment. The Dragon had been landed!

Wide eyed, I stared right into the face of a 50-pound Common Snapping Turtle. With its mouth agape, exposing its brilliant pink tongue, I realized that its bolt-cutter-like jaws were wide enough

to hold my entire forearm. It was an unbelievably impressive animal who with a single bite could have easily taken my hand; so I wisely kept a safe distance, preventing a possible strike.

The animal was dripping with thick mud and looked as if it had just been unburied from the time of the dinosaurs. My eyes had never seen anything so incredible... so prehistoric. Admiring its inch-long claws and scale-covered forearms, I stared down the length of its dome-like shell, which was alive with squirming leeches. I then walked around behind it to admire the saw-like ridge of the shell which I had so desperately clutched. The tail curled alongside its body was massive, at least a foot in length; it was the closest thing to a living dinosaur that I had ever seen. I flexed my hands and stretched my fingers; they were sore, exhausted, and battle-worn. The mud beneath my fingernails had been driven so deep that they throbbed in pain, while the laceration from the dragon's claws spilled blood down my thumb and onto the golden grasses around me.

I was exhausted, covered in mud, and standing bootless. The sun was quickly disappearing behind the trees, but I didn't care. I collapsed to the ground and sat a couple feet from the turtle. In that moment of truce its mouth closed and its body relaxed. We both calmed our breathing and stared at each other with bewildered eyes; mine infatuated with his elegance and perfection, his probably with the thought of...

"How in the world did this little kid ever catch me?!"

The turtle then exhaled again, the sound resonating deep in my chest as the beast then lifted its massive body up off the ground and onto all four feet. It startled me. I had never seen a turtle walk like that before, and I shuffled backward a few feet in the grass. The Dragon slowly turned back toward the lake, telling me it was time to return. I watched as he slid down the embankment and splashed into the water. I stood up, and as I did the giant turned his head back and looked right at me, those golden diamond eyes,

as ancient as I had always imagined they would be, looking right into mine and saying,

"Well done, you actually did it." In what seemed like slow motion, it slogged into the water, and I watched while the mud swallowed its shadow as the turtle disappeared back into the abyss.

Twilight had passed, the meadow was growing dark and as I stood there soaking wet with mud and sweat, I looked down at my bloodied hand to admire the would-be scar that the Dragon had bestowed upon me. A smile beamed across my face, and in that moment, I knew that I wanted nothing more in my life than to get up close with as many animals as I could.

I turned toward home and began to make my way back through the meadow. It took me all summer, but I had finally done it, I had captured *The Dragon*. And while no one was around to witness my incredible triumph, I just hoped that my mom would believe the incredible reason why I was coming home... without my boots.

Chapter 2

Rogue Buffalo

O ne of the greatest things about being 15 years old is that you feel as if you are old enough and brave enough to do anything. This is the mindset which propelled me forward as I continued my search for incredible animal encounters into my early teens.

Worn leather hiking boots laced tightly to my feet matted down tall yellow prairie grasses as I veered off trail and began to explore a world that I had never imagined I would set eyes upon. Welcome to Wyoming, one of the most epic wilderness landscapes in North America, where massive white clouds roll across an endless sky and distant mountains paint the horizon like jagged teeth breaking out of the earth's surface.

For a moment, I stopped and closed my eyes to soak in this untamed beauty. A gentle wind caused the long flowing grasses to dance as my outstretched fingertips touched their feathery tufts, reminding me of the serenity of nature. I was in complete and total harmony with my surroundings; I was at peace.

As I slowly opened my eyes, a smile cracked upon my face; this was about to be one epic adventure, yet in that moment I had no idea that it might also be my last.

My Mom and younger sister were back at our base camp, where our metallic silver 1988 Chevy Suburban was parked in the shade of a towering old tree. This was our cross-country chariot, and hitched to it was our home on the road: an old white and teal Scotty Sportsman trailer. To a 15 year old it was a dream home, though to a discerning adult it was barely enough space to fit three small people. However, to us size didn't matter – we had been having the time of our lives for the past several weeks as we gallivanted across the northern edge of the United States. From Ohio to Michigan, down through Indiana, across Illinois and back up through the vast open wilds of Iowa and South Dakota, each and every state was a wonder to behold; but nothing was as breathtaking as Wyoming.

Many of the greatest memories from my childhood came from the cross-country adventures my Mom used to take our family on. I was seeing and experiencing things most children my age could never even imagine. The best part was that my Mom trusted me to always make smart, safe decisions when I was out adventuring on my own in nature.

Let's be honest here for a minute, at 15 years old, your decisions are often about as risky as they get. The moment I told her I was headed out onto the prairie to search for rocks and wild artifacts, or land "treasure" as I called it, I knew in the back of my mind that finding danger was inevitable. In fact, I was chomping at the bit to put myself up against any challenge that would push the bounds of my own bravery.

This was definitely my mindset as a teenager.

As I walked slowly through the prairie grasses, I carefully scanned the environment for any signs of animals. This was the perfect place to find rattlesnakes and whip-tailed lizards, or maybe if I was lucky enough, a snarly badger defending its burrow. How I would have loved to see a badger in the wild, despite the fact that I

knew if you tangle with a badger, you are likely going to walk away shredded to bits.

In the distance, I could see a beautiful range of mountains, the rocky peaks reaching for the sky and the sun casting a warm glow down that seemed to draw me toward them. I was well off the trail now, and the last thing on my mind was how far I had gone. With each step, my curiosity drew me further from camp with a natural wonder for what was next beyond the bend.

The landscape quickly began to change, as scraggly bushes now littered the path forward and forced me to twist and turn my advancing direction. It was like a maze of obstacles – I battled the increasingly difficult terrain until I came upon a steep wash that cut through the prairie. My boots inched forward cautiously toward the edge and I peered over.

"Great, not much choice here," I thought to myself... "it's either climb down, through, up, and over OR turn around and head back to camp so I can hang out with my annoying little sister!"

"Ugh... NO WAY!" I said to myself. And before I knew it, my butt was in the dirt and sliding down the brittle side of the wash.

Parched earth began crumbling under my boots... The hillside broke apart and quickly began to slide me down with it into the wash. I was caught up in a skeet slide, and I thought to myself, "This is bad news bears!" My heart began to race as rocks dislodged around me and I battled to keep my balance. I was moving as one with the earth now, and a single wrong move could find me buried under a pile of falling rocks. I dodged left and back right, my ankles fighting to keep from twisting as the uneven ground attempted to contort my stance and crumble me to the dirt. This was my moment, live or die, and with a confident leap I sprang from the hillside and luckily made my landing in the middle of the wash.

POOF! A plume of dry dust enveloped me as rocks rolled to a stop at my feet. I dusted off my shorts and shirt, took a deep breath, and looked around.

"WHOA! That was awesome, like, way past cool!!" I wished someone had seen me pull that one off.

I jumped around in excitement, my adrenaline at its peak, and then I realized that this was a very dangerous place to be standing. In the event of a sudden rainstorm, flash flooding could come rushing down this wash and sweep me away. There was no point in tempting fate, so I decided to take on the challenge of scaling the opposite side of the wash. With a couple of clever moves, using rock outcrops, some protruding roots, and sheer determination, I shimmied up and out the far side of the wash. I took a deep breath, exhaled, and there I stood, a victor.

I had mastered my obstacle, and laid out before me was nothing but the unknown. I took one more look back in the direction I had come from. The camp was nowhere in sight. Even if I screamed for help at the top of my lungs right then and there, no one would be able to hear me. Boy, was I a long way from camp; I started to wonder if Mom was getting worried.

Standing there in the radiant sun, I began to question my mission.

"Should I head back? Have I come far enough? I haven't seen any animals yet. I didn't find any land treasures." If I returned with only the story of making the descent down a wash, my little sister would most certainly giggle and say, "Ooh so brave, you slid down some rocks... I could have done that... in my SLEEP!"

I refused to be the subject of her snickering, so I trudged onward out across the shrub-scattered prairie. I was not going to return without something worthy of a grand tale. Something epic was bound to happen; it was Wyoming for Pete's sake, the Wild West! I would have taken anything at that moment.

"Come on nature... present me with something epic!"

With my head down, I was more focused on the thoughts in my head than I was on the surrounding environment, a definite mistake whenever exploring unknown wilderness. I moved quickly, dodging around spiky plants that laced the tall grasses, and kicking at the small rocks that scattered the sandy soil. My frustration was clearly apparent, and it was growing with every step I took.

I picked up my pace. The faster I moved, the less I was paying attention to everything around me, and the danger was compounding.

"No snakes, no lizards, no fossils... shoot, not even a prairie dog standing on its back feet to call out a chatter of laughter which would most

certainly be mocking me as I..."
My thoughts froze as all of a sudden the bushes ahead of me
moved with incredible force. I stopped dead in my tracks.
Like a video game freezing in mid-play, my entire world
literally stopped.

Branches cracked back and snapped, the entire bush moved
violently, yet I could not make out what was behind it. One thing
was for certain – it was BIG.

This was one of those rare moments in life where you can literally
feel your heart drop in your chest. Your senses shift into overdrive
and begin firing on all cylinders to pump as much adrenaline
through your veins as possible.

"Buh-bum... buh-bum... BUH-BUM..."

My heart was pounding out of my chest as my ears tuned in and
listened to the haunting sound of deep breathing coming from in
front of me, no more than 50 feet away.

I heard a low resonating bellow, like distant thunder... the sound
rumbled into my chest, and then suddenly a short, strong snort
caused me to jump. It was the sound of air being forced through a
pair of nostrils, a crystal clear warning that said:

"I am here and *YOU* should *NOT* be!"

My body was paralyzed by fear, yet my mind was screaming at my
feet, "RUN, COYOTE, RUN!"

But they could not hear my internal cries
of desperation. My heart began to race
faster as the sound of crunching
sand and stone echoed out across
the open landscape. Stepping
out before me the beast revealed
itself, arguably the most powerful and
dangerous animal to roam the grasslands;
the American Buffalo.

To say he was absolutely enormous is an understatement.

His massive head was armed with curved black horns that led into a muscle-packed neck. My eyes traced up his haunches and across his massive shoulders, burly and coated in thick tufted fur. His powerful ground-pulverizing hooves braced as they held up a 2,000 pound core. This animal was like a freight train on legs, capable of reaching speeds of nearly 40 miles per hour.

He looked straight at me, his eyes like two black marbles glistening in the late afternoon sun, almost lost in the dark traces of his brow line and filled with a timeless wisdom. This animal represented dominance and power. This land belonged to him, yet here I was, trespassing in his domain.

What an incredibly rare moment – partially because I had not yet been charged or trampled, but also because it's rare to ever see a buffalo outside of a herd. Normally these giant herbivores travel together by the hundreds, and you will only find a rogue male who has been driven out of the heard in a situation like this.

My current predicament had become incredibly dangerous, because it was clear that this buffalo was NOT happy. Large, aggressive rogue males are notorious for charging humans. Most of the time it's a tourist who has gotten too close while trying to snap a photograph; this time it was a tourist who foolishly wandered haphazardly across a prairie looking for an adventure.

Now, I knew the worst thing I could do in this situation was to run. If I ran, it would most likely prompt a charge, and there was no way whatsoever I was going to outrun a buffalo. At top speed, an adult human can sprint around 15 mph. And remember, a full-grown buffalo... about 40 mph. You can see the impossible nature of attempting to outrun this beast. However, I had already made the mistake of direct eye contact, so at this juncture, I was already in way over my head!

"Think Coyote… think, how are you going to get out of this one…?"

My thoughts were cut short as suddenly he snorted again!

"WHHHUUUGGHHHHHH"

A massive burst of air and snot shot from his nose and sent up a plume of dust from the ground. My head immediately dropped, and I looked at my feet. I noticed my knees were now shaking from fear and I closed my eyes.

"He's gonna charge," I thought. "He's gonna charge, and he's gonna kill me if I don't back myself out of this now… right now!"

I slowly opened my eyes and somehow mustered a single small step backward, my boots crunching ever so loudly on the ground; the sound seemed to echo across the prairie, and I stopped.

The buffalo exhaled again, and with a mechanically powerful movement his front left hoof pawed at the parched earth; a burst of dust kicked up as he displayed his dominance. The king of Wyoming had just signaled that this prairie belonged to him, and boy, I could not agree more. I would have gladly apologized – perhaps in a fashion something like this:

"Gosh, I'm sorry Mr. Buffalo… I was just out looking for snakes and lizards. I didn't realize this was your side of the wash. I certainly would never have wanted to offend a handsome fella such as yourself. What do you say I head back to the human camp and we forget this whole thing ever happened?"

Yeah… unfortunately, that wasn't going to work.

If the giant charged, it was likely to cover the space between me and itself in less than 10 seconds. The force of a 2,000-pound freight train would run me over like I was a single blade of prairie grass; my trampled bodily remains would likely become an evening feast for a wake of turkey vultures.

Suddenly, sticking around camp to help my Mom and sister make dinner sounded like a really good place to be!

I took another calm and collected step backward; the buffalo... did not move.

With my eyes pointed straight at the ground, I took one more. No reaction from the great American icon. In fact, he seemed disinterested as he licked at his nose with a long gray tongue; the slurping sound of wet muscle on slimy nostrils was loud and gross. I watched from the corner of my eye as his long tail methodically swatted at the barrage of flies that swarmed his massive stature.

"This was good" I thought. "Maybe he is angry at the flies, maybe he didn't even notice me... how great would this be, saved by flies... who would have ever imagined that?"

I took another step, then another... and another. My heart rate began to even out as my distance from immediate danger was growing with...

And then it happened!

"OH... MY... CRAP!"

For reasons unknown to me, the rogue buffalo decided... IT WAS TIME TO TRAMPLE A COYOTE!

Like a freight train that had exploded from its tracks, this massive animal was charging at me full steam ahead; with no hesitation I turned around and ran like I had never run before.

Everything went black.

It was as if I were running in a dream state and the rest of the world had shut down around me. My heart was beating a million beats per second as my skinny tan legs cut through the prairie grasses, desperately trying to avoid tripping. The ground was shaking under rapidly-gaining hooves as the sound of an angry buffalo barreled down after me. For every stride I gained, he closed the gap by ten. I could practically feel the hot steam from his wet nostrils on the back of my neck, his rugged earth-worn hooves nipping at my heels, and the bone-crushing force of his iron-strong skull inching closer to slamming into my back.

This was the fastest I had ever run in my life, and to this day I am not sure I have ever covered ground more quickly. You would be surprised how fast you can run when your life literally depends on it!

Sweat poured from my brow as the dry air stung my eyes and open mouth. I gasped for air as my lungs worked on overdrive to propel my body forward... and then I saw it:

THE WASH!

The very environmental feature I had recently been so proud to have conquered might now be the only thing that could save my precious little life.

The buffalo was closing in; I could almost hear its heart beating as it blazed across the prairie.

"Just a few more yards... maybe if I jump I can make it to the other side..." and suddenly with all of my might I leapt from the edge and WOOOOOOSH!

Time seemed to slow in the following moments as my body launched off the side of the wash. My arms and legs flailed as I soared through the air, my eyes wide as saucers. The sound of the charging buffalo mixed together with the sound of wind in my ears as I flew toward the far side. I was flying, I couldn't believe it... I was literally flying!

And then... reality snapped back and my 15-year-old body fell like a ton of rocks, flat into the bottom of the wash. WHAAAAM!

I hit the sand and gravel with a cracking SLAM! The wind in my lungs was knocked straight out of me as my palms and knees smashed into the ground. In a sliding tumble, I rolled and skidded to an incredibly painful halt.

You see, the wash spanned about 25 feet across. Leaping from one side to the other... NOT humanly possible.

"Uhhhhh, uhhhhh, uhhhhh..." I moaned as my body squirmed in pain.

I struggled to regain my breathing and slowly rolled onto my back. Had I died? Had the buffalo trampled me? My eyes stared up into the blinding sun, white orbs spinning around in my head as I lay there in a daze not knowing what had just happened.

Blood oozed from my hands as they wrenched in pain. My knees were scraped and skinned many layers down, sand and stone painfully wedged into them. I winced in pain but caught my breath, finally realizing that I was not dead. This was great! ... except for the fact that I was in a serious world of hurt.

I looked up toward the far edge of the wash. No huffing, bellowing, or angry breathing. No hoof stomping. No trace. No... BUFFALO. I had just outrun certain doom by the hooves and horns of a great American icon, and as I lay there in temporary paralysis I began to cry tears of joy that I was still alive.

Well, tears of joy for being alive, but also tears of pain from the many cuts and scrapes I had suffered. "UGHHHHH!" I cried out as I slowly sat up and struggled to my feet. Blood poured down my knees, and I turned in a circle, coming to grips with what had just happened. I wiped the tears from my cheeks, took a deep breath, and fought my way back up the safe side of the wash.

When I made it to the top, I looked back, but the Rogue Buffalo was nowhere to be seen. Like a phantom, it had vanished amongst the shrubs and shadows, with not a single trace remaining. I slowly limped back toward camp, the sun now beginning to sink in a sky painted in a beautiful scene of cotton candy pinks, oranges and blues. I kept looking back over my shoulder, thinking I would hear the charging hooves of the animal that had chased me off the side of a cliff, yet saw nothing but grasses dancing in the wind.

Did that really just happen? Was I just chased and did I somehow outrun the most iconic mammal to ever roam Wyoming? YES. Yes, I did!

After arriving back at camp, broken and bruised, bloodied but breathing... my Mom cleaned me up as I recounted the tale. My encounter had been as grand as they come, and as my sister listened with wide eyes, she certainly had nothing to say other than...

"I am glad you're still alive!"

Chapter 3
King of the Everglades

I was always told to never grow up, and while I could not elude the passage of time and the perpetually aging body we are all given, at 30 years old, when I peered down at my own reflection in the water I still looked at myself as a child. Sure, my baby soft face was now rugged with a stubbly five o'clock shadow, and my physical stature had morphed into a formidable adult figure, yet, in my heart and soul I hadn't aged a day since capturing The Dragon.

As I placed my hands, scarred from years of adventure, down into the swamp, they distorted my reflection and I pulled a cupped wave of stagnant water over my face.

Welcome to the Florida Everglades, where the humidity is thick enough to cut with a saber and the flying insects are as relentless as gravity. Most would think that a splash of grimy swamp water would be the last thing one would want to relieve the afternoon heat, but trust me when I say it was the greatest feeling in the world.

In that moment, I was free. I was once again one with the elements of nature, and as the water trickled off my chin, I pictured myself in command of this foreign land, yet in actuality... I was far from being king.

The sun was inching past the three o'clock hour, and our time on this expedition was running out. Welcome to my first shoot of **Breaking Trail**, a new animal adventure series that my team and I had conceptualized, pitched to a network, and been given the green light to start capturing on camera.

This particular mission was simple: Catch an American Alligator... with my bare hands.

Yep, you read that right. Our first mission was to catch the most dangerous predator in the Florida Everglades... and I was going to do it without the use of any nets or traps.

As you can tell, **Breaking Trail** was envisioned with grand plans to encounter and get the cameras incredibly close to some serious predators. The good news for me was that I wasn't alone.

Let me introduce you to my crew, a camaraderie of brave individuals who will appear in chapters from here on in.

These guys were solid. The kind of friends and determined adventurers who like me, were willing to risk life and limb to get the best shots possible. Mark was our director; fearless, cunning, and driven beyond all odds to get the impossible through the eye of a camera lens. Then there was Chance, a jack of all trades who could not only run and gun a camera with the best in West Hollywood, but also an avid outdoorsman who could MacGyver a campfire... from a stick of gum, some pine needles and the nine volt battery out of his headlamp. Last, but certainly not least, my main man Mario. A wildlife biologist who had an incredible knack for not only helping me spot and identify wildlife, but who also had my back in the event that any animal encounter went awry. If there was one person I trusted to defuse a perilous wildlife situation, it was Mario.

This was my team, and together we were a band of wilderness cowboys. We loved and respected the environment, its plants, animals and above all else, its challenges. If anyone could take on the Everglades and go toe-to-tooth with its most notorious predator, it was us. The only problem was locating one of these reptilian powerhouses amidst the fields of razor sharp saw grass and endless waterways.

Ever heard the phrase, "it's like finding an alligator in saw grass?" Well, you have now, and trust me when I say it's not much easier than finding a needle in a haystack.

As our boots trudged through ankle-gobbling muck, I could sense the exhaustion falling upon us. Beads of sweat ran like waterfalls down the backs of our necks, and every next mosquito bite literally sucked the life from our progress. We had seen several alligators already that day. Some measured around four feet in length; a respectable reptile by all means, and an animal that commands respect. However, my goal was to encounter and capture one that measured closer to eight feet and that would likely weigh around 200 pounds.

I know what you are thinking: 'Coyote, a single person can't capture an eight foot, 200 pound alligator with their bare hands. You would need to use a snout rope, a net, and three fully grown, burly men to hold it down. Not only does this "catching it by hand" sound impossible, the very thought is complete madness!'

I agree with you. This was madness, but I was on a mission. I had everything to lose, and everything to prove. Not only to myself, but also to a network that had given my friends and I the chance of a lifetime to make the next big animal adventure show. I was going to do this, or at least I was going to go down trying.

As we cut across the open soggy plains of Southern Florida, I pictured myself as an early settler. I wondered if seeing this land 100 years ago would have been any different: great egrets perched in the trees, giant locusts dangling from the seeded tufts of reeds, and a strangely pure clarity to the swampy water we were currently slogging through.

For our life goals, we all find ways to challenge ourselves, and we are all each responsible for following the dreams that drive us. It was this very philosophy that had placed me smack in the middle of the Everglades' timeless expanse of wilderness.

From just a few feet to my left, Mario called out, "Got a moccasin over here... a big one!" We crept up slowly, and sure enough, coiled on a mound of dead saw grass was one of the most dangerous biological landmines we could have stumbled upon, the Florida Water Moccasin. These snakes can be incredibly aggressive if provoked or accidentally stepped on, and a single bite can put enough venom into a human body to cost the victim a limb and possibly even his or her life.

Mario backed up the camera

team and instructed us to alter our route. Little did we know at the time that encountering this snake and Mario's decision to change our direction would lead us down a fated path for which we had long been searching.

Mark and Chance carefully followed behind me. I knew what they were thinking. That was a big, venomous snake. I could see their gears grinding; they were on edge as each squish of their boots into the muck, just a foot below the water's surface, was taken with precision and care. It's important to take your time when exploring in nature because you never know what sort of biological landmines you may run into next.

So, what exactly is a biological landmine, you may ask?
Great question!

A bio-landmine is what we as a team have come to define as any plant or animal in the environment that one may accidentally stumble upon and that has the potential to do harm. From snakes, spiders, and scorpions to sink mud, cacti, and poisonous plants, nature is full of hidden dangers.

The potential peril of bio-landmines should never be taken lightly, but I was confident that in my heightened state of awareness, nothing could stop me from achieving our goal. While the crew was busy considering the possible dangers of the landscape we were venturing across, my mind was focused on one thing... finding an enormous alligator.

The clouds stretched across the horizon were epic, and as the dying sun began to illuminate them from a steep angle, a vast golden glowing hue became our backdrop. As I rounded a thick growth of cattails, meshed with saw grass and shrubs, my heart began to beat faster as a feeling in my chest told me that we were not alone.

Perhaps you know the feeling? You can find it in the shadows of your closet, or in the mystery of what's lurking under your bed. You cannot define it, but you know that something unseen is there... and it terrifies you.

That is when we saw him, partially submerged in an isolated pocket of water, his gnarled hide protruding from the surface and glistening in the warm colors of the setting sun. We all stood still as our eyes traced up the animal's back, toward its massive and prehistoric looking head. You never forget the first time you make eye contact with an American Alligator. Those dark bronze eyes set high up on the skull, lifeless and waiting for any unsuspecting animal to wander close enough to its snare-like jaws, clenched shut and armed with nearly 80 teeth. A single bite from this animal is powerful enough to crush bone.

We were in awe… and he was incredible. A Godzilla of ancient proportions, he was nearly ten feet in length and around 300 pounds. This was exactly the encounter I had been dreaming of all day!

"This is it! Here we go!" I cried out, as my confident voice became the first sound to break the frozen tension.

Mark looked at Chance; they both looked at Mario.

"Coyote's got this, I know he does!" Mario convinced them with a simple statement without an ounce of hesitation in his voice. In that instant Mark began to direct the team. Chance got into position a safe distance from the reptile and the cameras began to roll. This was my moment. I took a deep breath, and then Mark called, "ACTION!"

I slowly moved in on the Alligator; he was dead still, and might as well have been a rotting log, exhibiting the perfect camouflage for an ambush predator. In fact, it was almost impossible to tell the animal was alive until I got within about 15 feet and he suddenly released a guttural bellow, signaling us that he was there and that we had better not mistake him for anything but the king of the Everglades. I stopped dead in my tracks as he slowly opened his mouth, revealing a massive snag of tooth-lined jaws. My eyes widened in awe as I turned back to the camera.

"The American Alligator has one of the most powerful bite forces on the planet, clocking in at almost 2,000 pounds per square inch, combined with the ability to thrash its powerful neck and body; which pretty much means that if this animal grabs ahold of you, whatever it has bitten... you will not be getting back!"

I returned my attention to the reptile and began my advance. Just a single step forward and the beast erupted with a violent thrash of its long muscular tail. WHOOSH! A wave of water sent us all staggering backward, Mark and Chance dodging the splash in a serious effort to keep the cameras dry from the deluge.

"WOW! Did you get that on camera?" I screamed.

The alligator was now in full defense mode as I bravely moved forward, testing its lunging ability. With arms outstretched, giving it a visual distraction, I sidestepped the scaled defender as it hissed and exposed its flat white tongue. Looking down toward its throat, I could only imagine how terrifying it would be to find myself being swallowed by an animal of this magnitude. Though fear not; alligators have no interest in eating humans and most attacks come from a case of mistaken identity. Under normal circumstances, these aquatic reptiles primarily feast on fish, turtles, small mammals, and birds, and while I certainly didn't fear being eaten, a bite from this animal could easily take my arm or crush my leg. There was no question about it, this was becoming the most dangerous animal encounter I had ever faced. I may as well have been gazing into the throat of a Tyrannosaur!

I turned back toward Mark to deliver my plan of approach and capture.

"The key to making this capture will be outmaneuvering the alligator. What I want to do is get the reptile to strike at me in one direction and then quickly move in the opposite direction to flank this beast and jump on its back. It's going to thrash like a bucking bronco, but I think the weight of my body will keep it in place. As long as I get my hands behind its neck, I can safely get the animal under control."

I bet right now you are saying to yourself, "Coyote, this really sounds crazy!" and trust me, it was!

I made a quick move to the alligator's left, and it swung at me with incredible speed. I leapt backward, narrowly missing a chomp from its powerful jaws. The alligator growled and whipped its tail around, sending forth another wave of water that soaked me from the neck down. I moved around to the right as it watched me with focused eyes, jaws still open exposing its flesh-ripping teeth.

My heart was beating out of my chest as I could feel that the opportunity to make a jump on the animal's back was near. I took a step forward, and WOOSH, another spin; this time the tail caught my leg with immense force, causing me to nearly lose my footing.

"WHOOOOO! That was a close one!" I cried out to the cameras, knowing that the following morning would bring with it the presence of one nasty bruise.

Wet and muddy, shaken but not stopped, I stepped back into the proverbial "ring." I was not going to give up that easily, and the king knew it. I began my next approach; the alligator held its ground, firmly poised to strike.

"Mario, any suggestions here?" I called out.

"He seems to be slower on his moves to the right. Fake him left, go right and make the jump - whatever you do, DO NOT hesitate. You got this, and when you are on him, hold on for dear life!"

You have to love Mario's advice: "Just hold on for dear life!"

My steadfast hand wiped over my brow; sweat, swamp water, and mud streaked my face. I was a warrior in my mind, but a novice in the world of wrangling alligators, and this was about to be one of the most foolhardy plays I would ever be guilty of making. I exhaled in confidence and moved in. A quick dart to my left, and the reptile lunged its head. As its jaws snapped with a loud pop, it closed its eyes and I saw my window. I spun on my inside pivot foot as my left boot twisted in the mud with the grace of a figure skater, and I completed my turn. I had faked the giant on his right side. Mario had called it, and in a leap of pure faith I threw my body straight on top of the alligator.

"ROOOORRRRAAAAHHHH!"

The King of the Everglades erupted like a volcano of scales, teeth, and muscle. Water and mud splashed in a tidal wave toward Mark and Chance. Their cameras were doused, the lenses speckled with debris, yet they held the frame and continued to capture footage. My hands grasped onto the neck of the alligator, its accordion-like muscles contracting as its head swung from left to right, jaws snapping, looking for any purchase on the fool who had just jumped on its back. Five feet of muscle-laden tail swung violently

in the shallow water, creating a slurry of mud and plants as the beast began to turn a circle with me on its back. I held on for dear life, knowing that a reptile of this size would tire very quickly and then become calm. At least so I hoped. The key is to just never let yourself fall off and into the strike zone of those bone-crushing jaws. I could feel the heave of the animal breathing as it spun another half circle and then, as if someone had flipped a switch, the King of the Everglades exhaled and relaxed.

Adrenaline coursed through my veins as my muscles worked on overdrive to hold this prehistoric creature in place. My eyes shifted toward Mark and Chance, then back to Mario. I exhaled with a sigh of relief.

"We're good, guys, I've got him! OK, move in slow, keep about ten feet back, and let's get this scene!" My voice was alive with excitement, I could not wait to tell the cameras about this incredible animal.

The facts rolled off my tongue with ease and grace. I felt poetic in this moment as I described the feeling of power in the animal's muscles, armored scales, and dinosaur-like tail. I examined its jaw structure and warned of its lethal bite force. I expressed my appreciation for this animal and its importance to the Everglades ecosystem, then lastly reminded everyone that these animals are best admired from a safe distance.

For nearly 15 minutes, I sat upon the back of an animal that has lived on this planet for over 180 million years; a true living dinosaur and the most perfect predator to call the Everglades home. I kept my hold on the beast's neck firm, but as my heart's pace calmed I could feel the animal breathing, and I focused to find its rhythm. Together we inhaled and exhaled, inhaled, exhaled; the warm swamp air rushing in through our nostrils and filling our lungs with life. To breathe the same air as the King was incredible, and my heart began to swell with nothing but respect for this amazing reptile.

Finally, the scene was "in the can", and it was time to call this one a wrap.

Now for getting myself back off the alligator, which can be just as dangerous as getting on. I knew that the safest route would be a quick roll to the backside and away from the potential swing of its jaws. With a deep breath, I signaled to the crew and counted down...

"1... 2... 3... GO!" In a burst of speed I rolled from the alligator's back, sprang to my feet, and exited the scene.

"WHOOOOO!" I exclaimed in disbelief. A flawless encounter. I had done it! I had just captured a nearly ten foot, 300 pound alligator with my bare hands. No nets, no traps, no problem!

We all stood back and watched as the alligator spun a slow circle, hunkered down in the muddy water, and resumed the same appearance he had presented upon our arrival. A lifeless log floating just above the water's surface, jaws closed, beaded eyes gazing and waiting for the next unsuspecting target.

Mark, Chance, and Mario began to break trail back toward base camp, and I called ahead, "I'll catch up, give me a second."

I took to my knees in the primordial ooze and took a long look toward the King of the Everglades. As he peered back at me with those timeless bronze eyes, I felt that for a brief moment we connected, with a shared appreciation and respect for the animals we both were.

I bowed my head and I said, "Thank you. You are the true king of this place."

The sky now glowed with the brilliance of red-hot lava as a blood-soaked sun sank toward the edge of sight and kissed the clouds on its way below the horizon. I caught up to the boys and we celebrated the encounter we had just experienced. Little did we know as we set off into the sunset that this would become the first episode of Breaking Trail... and so the adventure begins.

Chapter 4

Capture Your Monsters

Growing up, we all have a monster that we fear. Maybe it's the one under your bed, covered in hair and spikes, with big snarly teeth backed by breath so rancid it could melt your favorite toy. Or perhaps it's the one lurking in your closet? You know what I am talking about. It loves the shadows and only seems to peek its glowing red eyes out when your parents turn off the lights and close your bedroom door.

Trust me, I have been there… the idea of monsters can be pretty scary, and I will be honest, visions of them have even haunted me. While I can tell you that they do not live under your bed or in your closet, there is a place where "monsters" do actually exist. That place… is called the Sonoran Desert.

Arizona's Sonoran Desert is one of the most beautiful places you can visit in the United States; yet it is one of the most difficult places for a camera team to film. Not only is it hot, but the terrain is laced with biological landmines, and there is absolutely no way

to avoid them all. In fact, your best bet is to hope that when you do step on one that it's only going to hurt and not send you to the emergency room!

It sounds extreme, I know. But it's the truth.

Everything, from the spine-covered Cholla cactus, to the Giant Desert Scorpion, Tarantula, and dare I say it, Western Diamondback Rattlesnake, lies in wait hidden amongst the craggy desert surface; get tagged by a rattler and you are in some serious, serious trouble!

It was only 7:00 a.m., and already the heat was intense. Sweat soaked the brim of my hat as I pulled my bandana from my pocket to wipe my brow. I was indeed overheated, but I was also nervous. I looked back at the crew; Mark, Chance, and Mario were lagging behind, and I didn't blame them.

"Come on guys, we need to cover some ground before the temperature reaches 100 degrees!" I called back to the team, motivating them to press forward. We only had a couple of hours to accomplish the mission, and when you are searching for a monster, every second counts.

My hiking boots crunched over sand and rock, leaving a wake of dust as I quickly rounded past prickly pear cacti and over the tops of scattered boulders. My focus shifted across every shadow cast by clusters of cacti, with extra care given to the mouths of the thousands of burrows that peppered the hillside.

One of these, and possibly many more, housed within them the only venomous lizard in the United States. It is a prehistoric relic measuring nearly two feet in length, covered in cryptic black and salmon-colored skin with eyes like tiny black marbles resting just above its jawline; a jawline filled with venom so powerful it's said that a single bite feels like hot lava coursing through your veins.

It sounds as if I have just described a creature from a horror film, I know, but the creature we were looking for was very real and none other than the Gila Monster!

'Hot lava coursing through
your veins?' I think you can
understand why I was just a little
nervous to be going after one of
these lizards.

Suddenly Mario, our wildlife
biologist, called out from the far
left of the group, "Coyote, I have a
bird's nest over here, and it's
been raided!"

"Mark, Chance... roll the cameras!" I barked as I was already
moving toward Mario's find. I slowed upon final approach and
quickly analyzed the scene. Sure enough, it was a quail's nest, or
at least... it used to be.

Mark dropped into position and called action on the scene, "rolling
Coyote." I turned to the camera and let my excitement fly.

"WOW, check this out! This nest has definitely been torn apart
and the eggs have been consumed. I can still
feel wet yolk on all of these discarded shell
fragments, and these tracks in the sand are
definitely reptilian in design. Look, here..." I
pointed down toward a tail drag in the sand.

"This is definitely evidence of a Gila Monster
and from the looks of it, a big one!" My eyes
were alive with excitement for the scene,
but on the inside, my heart was racing with
nervousness. We were now hot on the trail
of a true monster!

We began to track the lizard across the soft,
sandy surface of the desert. "Spread out, guys,
keep your eyes sharp and on the shadows – if the
lizard gets near a burrow it will disappear in a
flash, so if you spot one, stay still and call it out!"
I was no stranger to tracking Gila Monsters and had

come across many in my lifetime; however, I had always admired them from a distance and had never actually captured one with my own two hands. This time things would be different because I had the camera crew... and Breaking Trail is not a series about seeing animals from afar, it's about getting up close and personal with them!

We followed the trail down a hillside and into a wash, which is considered an animal superhighway. Washes are formed in low areas of the desert from torrential monsoon rains, and they clear everything in their path. Picture a web of roadways made of sand crisscrossing right in the middle of the desert. They're super easy to navigate and are used by nearly every type of desert animal, from snakes and lizards to spiders and rodents, to travel across the terrain. Their open nature allows you to clearly see anything that is moving down or across them.

I knelt on a single knee and examined the lizard's trail. 'Where would I go if I was a Gila Monster?' I thought to myself. 'Easy, I'd go right in front of the cameras so that I could give Coyote the chance to face his fears and the crew an awesome scene!' Ha... wishful thinking is called wishful thinking for a reason. I quickly snapped back to reality.

It was obvious that the lizard had gone straight across the wash. I could see the scamper lines, and in my mind I pictured its clawed feet propelling its long sluggish body forward, up over the far edge of the wash, and back up the hillside into the cacti clusters.

I sprang to my feet and quickly rushed across the wash, dodging a barrel cactus while pulling the binoculars from my hip. A glimpse of movement had captured my attention, and I dropped to my knees, keeping myself low to the ground and hidden from possibly being seen. A rush of excitement began to churn in my stomach as I slowly lifted the

binoculars to my face. Sweat seeped down my brow and into my eyes as the pressure of the binocular cups pressed tightly to my face. I squinted and adjusted the focus until the lenses went clear. I drifted my head to the right and then back left, when suddenly I stopped.

"Guys... guys... I've got a MONSTER, about 50 feet ahead of us, right in front of a prickly pear cactus, and it's big!"

Mark and Chance crept up slowly and prepared the cameras, double-checking their battery life and ensuring their lenses were clean and that microphones were on. It was go time! If I could move like a shadow in the wind, I might be able to sneak up and around the lizard to block it from escaping into the burrow that was no more than 3 feet behind it.

My heart was speeding on overdrive, my nerves firing out of control. This was about to be one of those monumental moments in my life. I was going to have to face my fear so that I could catch a real living monster. This was absolutely crazy... but it was happening!

"Okay Mario, you come with me. I need you to act as a visual distraction if the lizard decides to make a dash for the burrow. As long as I can get between the monster and the mouth of the escape hatch before he does, I am confident I can make a safe catch."

Mario is an excellent wildlife biologist, not only because he knows just about everything there is to know about animals, but also because he is always keen on reminding me of the dangers.

"Coyote, no matter what happens, do not get bitten. If he strikes and he gets you, he will lock on like a bulldog, and we are a long way from a hospital, my friend."

"Copy that!" I replied with confidence, despite the fact that there was nothing I feared more than taking a bite from this lizard!

I instructed the crew to slowly move alongside me and we began our approach.

We stayed low to the ground, doing our best to hide behind any natural barriers we could; so far, the lizard was completely unaware of our presence. Mario had flanked to the right as we circled the lizard to the left, and we were now closing in on the reptile. I refused to blink as beads of sweat poured down my jawline and traced the arch of my neck. Then... the monster lifted its head. I put my hand up toward Mark and Chance, signaling them to freeze. We all watched with nervous eyes.

The lizard flicked out its long, black, forked tongue, tasting the air. It was smelling the environment; something had caught its attention. I hoped it was just licking quail yolk from its lips from this morning's feast. A well-fed lizard is a lazy lizard, and if it was stuffed to the brim, its escape speed could be considerably slowed.

Another flick of the tongue and a slight turn of the head, it was looking right at us... I mean right at us. I could see the glare of the sun reflecting off its black eye, and we all remained frozen. This was it, that rare moment when the predator becomes the prey, and it knew it.

I once learned that hesitation only results in missed opportunities, and despite my nerves telling me otherwise, without waiting a second longer, I sprang into action. I already knew the cameras were rolling, and the boys know that when I spring... they had better follow.

My boots flew across the rocky desert surface, and by the time I had made my first stride, the lizard was already in action, scampering toward the darkness of the burrow; its home, its safe haven.

"Mario, GO!" I screamed for his assistance, and like a roadrunner out of left field, he leapt from behind a cactus, threw his hands in the air, and shouted, "HEY, LIZARD!"

The visual distraction worked, and the Gila Monster reared its head, opened its massive jaws, and spun toward Mario and away from its escape route. The reptile hissed and stood its ground, its black gums and tongue exposed to the hot desert sunlight, glistening a warning of venomous pain. I was closing in, and with a sliding leap I created a barrier between the burrow and one very angry monster.

Mark and Chance kept a safe distance; with both cameras rolling, they captured the excitement and the action as it played out. Mario gave me the nod that he was stepping back, as clearly the scene was now mine to execute. I addressed the cameras as I prepared to face my fears... it was time to capture the monster.

"Ok guys, now if there is one thing I have to stress, it's that you NEVER, and I mean NEVER, want to try and capture a Gila Monster like I am about to attempt. A bite from this animal is incredibly painful and potentially deadly, so if this goes wrong, it's going to be a very, very bad day for Coyote."

I was nervous, beyond nervous, but I forced myself to clear my mind of fear and focus on the task at hand. These were the moments when I often performed best – high risk with hefty reward. However, even the slightest slip-up, and that reward would become a lesson you wouldn't wish on your worst enemy.

As I slowly moved in, the lizard could immediately tell that I was getting too close for comfort, and it reared around with a hiss and a snap of its jaws. Oh boy, it was snarly! The burrow was still about three feet away, but I had a plan.

If I moved away from the burrow and opened up an escape path, maybe it would calm down, close its jaws, and make a run for safety. This would allow me to quickly sneak in behind it and make a catch by grabbing the neck just behind the head. A crazy move, but the only safe place to grab hold of a venomous lizard.

I presented the plan to the cameras and slowly stepped to the side, calmly talking to the lizard, assuring it that we were not there to do it any harm. We just wanted to admire it and educate the world for a few minutes while we filmed the scene.

The lizard closed its jaws and relaxed its body, its breathing balanced... THIS WAS IT! I dove headfirst, and with laser precision I grabbed ahold of the Gila Monster – A PERFECT GRAB! Right where the neck connected to its head, my hold was firm yet considerate and in just the right spot to keep both the lizard and myself out of harm's way!

The monster's powerful body wriggled and fought as its claws dug at the ground, trying to make purchase so it could break free and escape into the darkness of its burrow. My elbows ached with pain from being stabbed with the fallen needles of prickly pear cacti, but I had done it. I had faced my fears and I had caught a real live monster!

"I GOT HIM GUYS, I GOT HIM!" The excitement from the team was electric and the scene began to roll. I presented the animal from tip to tail, highlighting the elegance of its armor-like beaded skin that not only protected it from predators, but also helped it to retain water during long dry spells in the parched Sonoran summers. The cameras zoomed tight to admire the bulging venom glands on the lower jaws, which harbored a death serum for any unsuspecting prey. Mark panned down the length of the lizard, and we studied its abnormally robust tail, which acts as an emergency food reserve of fat in the event that the desert runs out of mice, other lizards, or quail eggs to eat.

From a distance, Mario watched and listened as I spouted off the facts he and I had spent hours reviewing; "The Gila Monster is the only venomous lizard in the United States. They're not typically very aggressive, and it's not very often that people are bitten by Gila Monsters; they say it is only a fool who mishandles a Gila Monster, and that ever receives a bite."

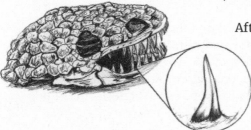

After pointing out the venom glands on the lizard's lower jaw, I described the process by which these Monsters deliver their painful bite. With rows of razor-sharp teeth, as opposed to a set of long fangs, "They gnaw and gnaw, working the venom into their saliva and ultimately into the wound of their victim."

At that moment, the lizard flicked its tongue, giving me the perfect lead-in to my next set of facts. "What's really interesting about its tongue is that it's forked just like a snake's. They run that over what is called the Jacobson organ in the roof of the mouth. That's like this lizard's personal computer that's bringing in all sorts of chemicals and processing information from potential prey, predators, and its environment."

"Gila Monsters are incredibly intelligent reptiles. They will often follow the trail of a mammal back to its burrow. If there are babies in the burrow, then he has lunch. If it is empty, he will remember the location and return several times until there is something inside to eat."

I was in complete awe of this animal, and as I ran my fingers along the lizard's skin, I admired its armor-like appearance. This animal was incredibly well adapted to surviving in a rugged ecosystem like the Sonoran Desert, and I described why it got its name from this unique feature.

"The scientific name for the Gila Monster, Heloderma, means nail-studded skin. All these little bumps running down his back are actually osteoderms, little pieces of bone covered in scale. This guy pretty much has bulletproof skin."

It was nearly time to wrap the scene, but I wanted to leave the audience with a warning when it came to getting up close with a Gila Monster in the wild and exactly why you should never try to handle one.

"If you're unfortunate enough to be bitten by a Gila Monster, it's going to be one of the most painful experiences you've ever gone through. The only way to get this reptile off you is to submerge it into a bucket of water. Once it lets go, remember this is a venomous animal and you're going to want to get yourself to the hospital as soon as possible."

I could tell Mario was proud as my presentation rhythm sang in the scorching sun. As humans, we were all cooking alive, but it was well worth it to spend this time in the presence of the Southwest's most notorious monster. These moments were exactly what we lived for, and this time around, the risk was definitely worth the reward!

I gave my closing thoughts to the camera, and as I turned the lizard toward the lens and spouted off my signature closing, "Be Brave, Stay Wild... We'll see you on the next adventure!" I gave the monster one last look. It was without question the biggest I had ever seen and a truly legendary first capture.

It was a jewel of the desert sands and a predator that, without a doubt, commanded respect. I gently placed it down just before the burrow and with lightning speed released my hold on the back of its neck. Without hesitation, the lizard quickly scampered through the mouth and disappeared down into the darkness, and just as quickly as we had seen it for the first time... it was gone.

Turning back to the crew, we all celebrated with a round of high fives, cheers, and water bottles. To say we were parched was an understatement, and like a victorious sports team, we all chugged down the lifesaving H2O. Water means everything in the desert; whether you are a native plant or animal or just a visiting human, you will lose your life without it.

The sun was now high in the sky and beating down with 110

degree temperatures; it was time to head back home. With the scene "in the can" and cameras packed up, our spirits were about as high as they could be.

In my mind, I reflected on the risk I had just taken, "Was it worth it... to take that leap of faith and make that capture? Is filming a scene like this for the world to see an even trade for the potential of a searing venomous bite?"

I knew they were good questions to ask, and while I certainly hoped that anyone who watched the episode would take heed of my warnings and never try to capture a Gila Monster, I was truly proud of myself. Because in one way or another, we all must face monsters at one time or another. Whether they live in our imaginations or within the mysterious world that is the Sonoran Desert, it's always best to just go for it, and face your fears head-on... because hesitation only leads to missed opportunities.

Chapter 5

Things That Crawl in the Night!

This is probably a good time to admit that when I was a kid, I was afraid of the dark. Yes, it's true; young Coyote Peterson had his very own frog night-light that illuminated the shadows and provided a warm comforting glow as he drifted off to sleep. The dark can be scary. After all, who knows what is lurking in the corners of the room, or in the far reaches of the basement? All I know is that when the sun goes down and the lights go out, our imaginations run wild...

In Arizona's Sonoran Desert, not only are the nights considerably cooler than the scorching days, but the cloak of darkness offers the ability for animals to move from spot to spot undetected on their search for food. Whether you are a small mouse collecting seeds or a stealthy rattlesnake out on the slither searching for the next unsuspecting prey, the nighttime is your best friend. Thus, once the sun goes down in the desert, the entire landscape is literally crawling with wildlife.

The piercing white beams of our headlamps illuminated the sand with a bright glow as our boots crunched across the desert. I led the team as we walked in a single file line, carefully navigating our way around barrel and prickly pear cacti. If you thought bio-landmines were tough to avoid by the light of day, just imagine trying to avoid them at night!

In case you forgot, a bio-landmine is what we as a team have come to define as any plant or animal in the environment that one may accidentally stumble upon and that has the potential to do harm. From venomous animals to poisonous plants, nature is full of hidden dangers.

I called over my shoulder to the team, "Everyone just move slowly, take your time, there is no rush. The last thing we want to do is step on a sidewinder rattlesnake or walk through the web of a black widow!"

I was half joking, but biological landmines were a very serious threat. Snakes, spiders, scorpions, and centipedes all canvas the desert at night, and your odds of encountering one, if not all of them, are pretty good.  This sounds horrible if you suffer from a case of arachnophobia; however, it was fantastic for an animal adventure team, as our goal was to find and film as many animals as possible.

In the forefront of my mind, one particular target was locked in, a creature that was capable of giving most people nightmares with its massive fangs and hairy legs. A creepy-crawly that could literally scale the side of your house or, even worse, your leg! It sounds like an animal you would want to avoid at all cost, however, I was confident that either we would find one... or perhaps, one would find us first!

I stopped dead in my tracks and held up my hand, signaling for the team to halt, as I barked back to Chance, who was operating the panel light.

"Hey, kill the lights for a second, I want you guys to see something."

We all turned off our headlamps and flashlights; the camera lights went dim. Suddenly the world fell into darkness; an incredible darkness so bleak it felt as if your eyes were already closed when they were actually wide open.

"Give it a second, let your eyes adjust." I called out.

I tilted my head back and looked up toward the sky, inhaling a deep breath of nighttime desert air. The dry smell of sand and the sweet aroma of my favorite native plant, the creosote bush, filled my nostrils, reminding me how much I loved the desert. Slowly my eyes began to adjust and as they did, the brilliant array of stars across the sky came into focus. Literally millions of little glowing orbs seemed to appear out of nowhere as we all admired the beautiful view of the Milky Way Galaxy.

No stargazing experience compares to standing in the middle of the Sonoran Desert at night; it's a visual gateway into the solar system and words cannot truly describe its epic nature.

"Whoa, a shooting star!", Mark called out. "Did you guys see that?"

All of us had. It was a sign of good luck and the nighttime telling us that it was time to move on. Standing in the darkness of the desert is a cool experience, but hang around too long and before you know it, a scorpion may be climbing up your pant leg!

We continued across the starlit landscape and made our way down the hillside before us toward a wash. If you remember, a wash can be viewed as an animal super highway that has been naturally created in the desert by monsoon rains. These dry streambeds winding through the terrain are often the perfect place to look for animals while safely avoiding bio-landmines. But as the old saying goes... never speak too soon...

"Nobody move, no... body... MOVE!" I slowly knelt toward the ground and tilted my head, angling my light beam into a web that had been cast between the side of a barrel cactus and some desert grasses. My eyes were alive with wonder, and I appreciated my reflex ability to quickly recognize a glimmer of spider silk in the shine of a light beam.

She was big, beautiful, and black as the night was dark. Her abdomen glistened as she spun around in her web, revealing her underside adorned with the iconic red hourglass marking. This was a bio-landmine superstar, the black widow spider! She had been spotted, and she knew it. The display of her hourglass symbol was a clear sign to any savvy outdoorsman that she was venomous and a bite could be incredibly painful. I immediately knew this was an encounter that we needed to capture on camera, so I called out to the crew.

1.5"

"Guys, let's get the lights up and roll the cameras on this one... it was a close call, I almost walked into her and it could have been the end of this adventure if she had bitten me!"

I was definitely feeling lucky at that moment. Walking through a black widow web doesn't usually result in an immediate bite. Their fangs are rather small, so biting through hiking pants or a shirt is relatively difficult, not to mention the fact that they don't have any real interest in biting humans.

black widow bites are often induced when you unknowingly walk through a spider web and the animal becomes displaced on your clothes. You keep walking, and as you do, the spider is also walking on you and it eventually makes its way to your neckline, up your collar and into your hair. Or maybe it finds that perfect moment to fall into your shoe, right where the ankle meets the sock line and WHAM; your boot steps funny, pinching the spider, and you are bitten!

The pain is immediate. Like a hot needle piercing your skin, it penetrates and it sears. In a panic, you flail at your leg and foot, smacking your boot, trying to eliminate the pain, yet the spider panics and you're bitten for a second time.

Only seconds have gone by, but already you have twice been tagged, and now the spider has either fallen off, or sadly, it has been squashed. Either way – your foot feels like it's on fire! The venom slowly works its way into your bloodstream, and as it does your heart begins to race with panic. You have just been bitten by a spider, you are in the middle of the desert, and now you cannot walk because your foot is swelling up like a balloon. Your fear radiates with terror as you realize this may be only the beginning of a truly horrific situation.

Hold on. Take a deep breath, and relax. I have some very good news. The black widow, though venomous and capable of giving a painful bite, has only very rarely been responsible for human fatalities. If you keep control of your heart rate, do your best to avoid panic and get yourself medical attention, you are most likely going to be just fine.

After presenting a brief scene about the spider and why you want to avoid it, we carefully walked around the web and off into the wash. I looked over to our wildlife biologist Mario with an expression of relief on my face.

"Whooooo, that was a lucky one, did you see how close I came to walking straight into that web!"

Mario agreed, "Oh yeah, I've run into a few of them while out doing research in South Florida. I've never been bitten, but it always gets your heart racing when one happens to end up on your clothes. I find that by simply staying calm, you can quickly find a stick, let the spider walk up onto it, and then set the stick gently back on the ground. Everyone walks away unscathed!"

Only Mario would be able to tell a story like that, and actually have it be true. But it was great advice: if you ever find a spider on your person, staying calm is always the best way to avoid scaring the arachnid and keeping yourself bite-free.

I looked left and then right; the wash was almost identical in both directions as my flashlight beam illuminated the flowing white sand, scanning it for a hint of direction.

"I don't know guys, what do you think… we could head up the wash, which would take us toward the mountains, or down the wash, which would send us deeper into the desert."

Mark, Chance and Mario all did the same thing, flashlights scanning from left to right. It was anyone's guess when it came to choosing a direction that would hopefully lead us to another animal encounter.

Suddenly a gust of wind lifted in the cool night air, catching the brim of my favorite leather cowboy hat and pulling it from my head. "Hey!" I shouted. I chased it a few feet, grabbed hold, dusted it off and plopped it back on my head. We all looked at each other. This was as clear a sign as we were going to get, and we all knew it. Down the wash it was! We spread out and began to search for more desert creatures.

One of the most difficult things about exploring at night is being able to balance the differences between lightness, darkness and, as I refer to it, the shadow zone.

In the direct beam of a flashlight or headlamp, you can easily illuminate anything in your path, and while this clearly lit area is ideal for finding animals, you also have the areas of complete darkness outside of the light's reach. For an animal, the darkness means safety, and if an animal can see a beam of light coming, it doesn't take them long to realize that an intruder is in the environment. This in turn causes them to quickly flee the scene, dodging the light for the safety of darkness.

Between the light and the dark, you have the shadow zone, which is made up of just enough light for the human eye to see, but also enough darkness for an animal to still feel hidden. I believe it's an art form to train one's eyes to see beyond the illumination of a flashlight beam and to split the difference between the light and dark. This coveted area of secrecy is what defines the shadow zone; and if an animal finds itself hiding here, it is likely to stay in one place and not flee.

The real trick is being able to train your eyes to look for any unnatural shape in the sand, up against a fallen mesquite tree limb or just behind the barbs of a barrel cactus. An unnatural shape is usually an animal hiding patiently in the shadow zone, waiting for the invader to pass by before carrying on with the rest of its night.

Rattlesnakes, banded geckos, kangaroo rats and even scorpions are students of the shadow zone. However, I personally consider myself a master, especially when it comes to identifying these very creatures that thought they were so cleverly hidden.

I crouched close to the ground on a single knee and directed my flashlight beam down the wash; 20 yards away, something glimmered in the white light, like diamonds in the night. I turned to Mark and whispered,

"You ready to roll?"

"Yeah, speeding" he replied. I called out to Chance next, "Hey, keep the light low for now, this is going to be cool!" Chance dimmed the main lights, and now only my flashlight illuminated the scene as I pointed down the length of the wash and began to present.

"Look down the length of my flashlight beam, right there in the middle of the wash, about 20 yards out... do you see it?"

Mark immediately responded to my questioning, "It looks like glass reflecting in your flashlight beam..."

"No, wait for it..." I said, keeping him and the cameras in suspense, when suddenly... IT MOVED and WE WERE IN ACTION!

"Oh, I've got a good set of eyes, get the light on, get the light on... I've got movement right here by this rock..." It was exactly what I was hoping we would come across that night.

The gang followed closely behind me, and as we closed in, the desert creature came into focus. It was big and hairy; its eight legs all seemed to move in an almost mechanical fashion as it calmly walked across the sand. This was a predator that would cause most who encounter it to quickly head in the opposite direction, and it was without question an animal that truly defines the concept of arachnophobia, the Desert Blonde Tarantula!

I carefully moved in behind the giant spider, who was nearly seven inches in diameter. Immediately it felt my presence as it stood tall on the tips of its legs and twitched its abdomen. This twitching is a warning to any potential predator that if you get too close, something is definitely going to happen. While black widows carry a red warning sign on their abdomens, tarantulas have the ability to warn predators by flicking urticating hairs from their abdomen, which are like shards of fiberglass that can get stuck in your skin, breathed in through your nose, or even worse, projected into your eyes. No matter where you take the hit, these hairs are incredibly irritating and painful, so the last thing I wanted to do was instigate a barrage of tarantula spines.

I looked toward the camera and explained the good news... "As long as I stay calm, the animal will stay calm." Tarantulas don't want to launch their urticating hairs; they only use them as a defense if absolutely necessary.

Mario had a great idea and called out from off camera, "Hey Coyote, you should let the spider slowly walk up onto your hand so that you can show everyone at home that tarantulas are nothing to be afraid of, even though they are big and scary looking!"

Ugh... Mario always has the craziest, yet most brilliant ideas! To be honest, the last thing I wanted to do was handle a giant spider. I wasn't afraid of spiders at all; still, having one crawl on your hands is a totally different story. But I knew it would make for some great interaction with the animal, and as long as I didn't apply any pressure to the spider, it shouldn't be provoked into biting me with its quarter-inch fangs.

Yes, you read that right, these spiders have fangs that are a quarter of an inch long, and they are used to pin and inject venom into their prey. Anything from a gecko to a mouse is fair game, and trust me when I say those fangs are nothing to mess with!

I took a deep breath and slowly put my hands out in front of the spider. Mark followed my every move with the camera, and just as the lens pulled focus onto the illuminated arachnid, it reached out with its front legs and stepped onto my hand.

My heart began to race. This initial contact meant no turning back, as I could feel the bristly little hairs on its legs crawling up and onto the palm of my hand. I looked out of the corner of my eye toward Chance as he clenched his teeth in anticipation. I could tell that his skin was crawling at the site of this. You see, Chance doesn't really care for spiders all that much, and while he certainly respects them, when it comes to making contact... he is without question an arachnophobe, and has a great fear of the 8-legged creepy-crawlies and their cousins.

I slowly began to lift my hand off the ground, the spider now completely covering the expanse of my palm and fingers.

"WOW – that is a big spider right there... That definitely gets your heart racing..." Now the desert blonde tarantula has no interest, at least so I was hoping, in biting humans. So as long as I remained completely calm and only made very small and slow movements, I would be just fine.

And then it happened. The tarantula decided it was time to climb a Coyote, and before I knew it, the fuzzy nightmare was on my wrist and making its way up the back of my arm.

This was one of those moments during an animal presentation that you can never really prepare for. I tried to keep my focus as I continued delivering lines to the camera.

"OK, nothing to be worried about... where is the spider now, guys?"I had completely lost sight of this creepy-crawly, and the last thing I wanted to have happen was for it to get into my shirt, panic, and give me a walloping bite. Now as I mentioned, they have enormous fangs; however, the good news is that their venom is no more potent than that of a honey bee. So, while a bite may be painful and absolutely terrifying, the after effects are very mild.

Mark directed Chance to swing the lights around behind me and signaled to Mario that he might need to step in and help me wrangle the spider back into the scene, but he checked with me first.

"Coyote, it's on your back making its way toward your head. I'm still rolling... Should we keep the scene going?" Mark asked.

I turned my head and contorted my body into the light so the cameras could see the spider. I could feel beads of sweat building on my forehead. I didn't have arachnophobia, but wow, was I nervous. I knew that I needed to stay calm and get this situation back under control. Cutting the camera now would result in totally breaking the flow of the scene, and this was such a rare moment with a giant spider crawling all over me that I voiced up and kept us going.

"Yes, keep rolling! Where is he? Is he off?"

Nothing gets your heart racing faster than to know that somewhere on your person a large spider is crawling about; worse, I couldn't see it. I kept telling myself that these arachnids very rarely bite, that is, unless they get startled or feel threatened. Keeping myself calm was absolutely necessary as the crew stood helplessly watching from behind the safety of their cameras.

Mark brought me up to speed on the current position of the spider.

"OK, it's moving over your pack now and toward the side of your body... oh boy, try not to move!"

Mark's tone alone told me that he was nervous, which meant that the spider must be in a precarious position. I was afraid that it might try to climb under my pack, thinking it was a place to hide from the lights and cameras. The danger of this would be that if I moved my position at all and my pack placed weight on the arachnid, it might inflict a defensive bite thinking it was going to be squished.

This was bad, this was really bad! I knew that before the spider got too comfortable I needed to make a move, so with a slight turn, I blocked the spider from wedging itself further between my back and my pack. Then I called out to the crew in panic.

"OK, where is the spider now?"

Before anyone could even answer me, I caught the creature's movement out of the corner of my eye. It was crawling down my ribcage and toward my hip. With my left hand, I reached across the length of my body and carefully began to coax it back toward the floor of the desert. Its long hairy legs skittered across my belt, over the knife holstered to

FANGS

the belt, and back onto the sand. The tarantula was back in the wash!

"Whoooo! All right, I feel a little bit better now," I exclaimed, and then gave an enormous breath of relief as I was thrilled to be spider-free.

In my mind, I had escaped one of the most nerve-wracking spider encounters of my life, and we had caught it all on camera! I was certain that after watching this episode, anyone who was even slightly afraid of spiders would most certainly have their skin crawling with the heebie-jeebies!

Mark quickly repositioned the camera and Chance relit the scene as I continued to spout facts about the desert dweller. It was amazing, almost as if the spider had crawled over me as a test, to see how I would react to its presence on my body, because for the next twenty minutes it stayed right there in the scene with us. I let it crawl back on my hands and even gently picked it up to show the cameras its impressive set of fangs; something that definitely took some nerve, but the spider was one cool customer and gave us an incredible performance.

Once we got our final shots, I gently set the tarantula back down on to the sand and delivered my outro which ended in one of my funniest 'goodbyes' to an animal we have ever had in an episode of Breaking Trail...

"See ya later fuzzy butt!"

With a few elegant strides, he walked out of the frame back into the darkness, and eventually disappeared into the night. I turned toward the crew with a smile on my face, and in that moment, we all knew that we had just captured the most incredible tarantula encounter imaginable in the eye of the camera.

These spiders are incredibly common in the Sonoran Desert, and if you are searching in the right place at the right time, there is a good chance you can come across one. However, it's important to remember that an animal such as a tarantula is always best admired from a safe distance, and even though their venom is very mild, a bite from those giant fangs is still extremely painful!

With the episode all wrapped up, we had a long hike back through the dark desert to our base camp, with plenty of bio-landmines that we could still stumble upon, so our guards would need to stay up despite our excitement. There are many things that crawl in the night, and it's probably fair to say that most of them come across as scary. Spiders, scorpions, and snakes are just a few, but the truth is that these animals travel, hunt, or hide under the cover of darkness because in actuality they are far more afraid of humans than humans should ever be of them.

So, if you are going to bed tonight and are thinking about turning off your frog night-light, or maybe telling your parents that the light in the hallway doesn't need to stay on tonight, I'd say go for it! Because if you harness your inner animal imagination, the darkness of night can be pretty illuminating!

Chapter 6

Dangerous Things...
Come in Small Packages!

I n life, we are all blessed with numerous obstacles, many of which can seem insurmountable at times; challenges that push us to the limits of our physical and mental capabilities, forcing us right up to the edge where we consider giving up. 'Just give up...' It seems so simple, so logical, except that if you are in a position to be facing such a difficult challenge, it means you have made choices that have led you to that very moment, the moment where you either take another step and keep going, or the moment where you give in and call it quits.

The Brave Wilderness crew is NOT a team that quits, and as the rain fell in what seemed like walls of water from the sky, we stood beneath a rocky outcrop wondering how we were ever going to complete this adventure.

Welcome to the jungles of Costa Rica. This breathtakingly beautiful country is part of the gateway between North and South America, and it proudly boasts being one of the most biologically diverse ecosystems on the planet. From its rolling plains and epic vistas in the north to its lush interior, made up of dense jungles and prehistoric-looking valleys, thousands of plant and animal species

inhabit this small stretch of land that forms a division between the Pacific Ocean and the Caribbean Sea.

However, the southwestern tip of the country is what we decided to explore on this adventure; a seemingly lost world known as the Osa Peninsula. This was a place that very few human feet had ever dared to navigate, and rightfully so. The terrain was not only rough and rugged but also laced with more biological landmines than anywhere the crew and I had ever been.

Don't believe me? Let's just list a few and you will quickly see why the Osa Peninsula tests almost every element of a human's mental ability to tolerate danger and possible doom.

Spiders. Countless species, many of which are enormous, like the web-building golden orb weaver. When I say enormous, I mean the full circumference of this arachnid can be as large as a salad plate! Sure, you can avoid spiders in webs simply enough, as long as you pay attention to where you are walking. But what about the brazilian wandering spiders that litter the jungle floors? Big, hairy and aggressive, they will not think twice about dishing out a bite if you get too close. Their venom is famed as being the most potent of any spider in these Central American jungles; it can lead to massive tissue loss from necrosis. Don't know what that is? Just do a simple google search, if you dare. If you are at all squeamish, I suggest you just take my word for it; you have been warned.

Not afraid of spiders? How about snakes? From the elegant beauty of the eyelash viper, which can often be found hanging from tree branches, to the infamous fer-de-lance, which can grow to nearly six feet in length and is armed with venom-wielding fangs so potent that a single bite can kill a human in a matter of hours.

Spiders. Snakes. We are just getting started, the list goes on and on.

Even the ants, nature's tiny little assembly line, mean serious business. Leaf-cutter ants roam the jungles by the millions, and bullet ants come equipped with a sting so painful it's said it feels as if you have been shot by a gun!

We were no longer in the United States... This was the jungle, and at this point in the adventure, we were many miles into its maze of massive tree trunks, tangling vines, and disorienting lightscapes.

Imagine yourself as one of the crew. If you were to stop dead in your tracks and spin in a circle, it would seem as if every direction you turned looked exactly the same. Every step forward felt as if you were being led deeper into an unknown labyrinth. Despite its promise of exotic wildlife and excitement, this particular adventure was terrifying.

I stepped from beneath the rocky overhang and looked up into the torrential rain; beads of water splashed like tiny water balloons onto my face, further soaking my already-drenched adventure gear. I looked back toward Mark, who had his camera inside of a rain jacket to protect it from the deluge, but I could see the red flicker of the recording light signaling that he was rolling so I addressed the situation with arms outstretched.

"Well... I guess this is why they call it the rainforest!"

The only thing we could do was wait and hope that soon the rain would subside, because turning around to head back to our base camp in those conditions was NOT an option.

Our departure from camp came just after sunrise and it had taken us nearly three hours to navigate the dense plant-tangled jungles, which were at times so thick that even the razor-sharp blades of our machetes couldn't cut a clear trail forward.

From there we made our way to the top of a massive ravine which had cut itself into the jungle with the precision of time and millions of years of erosion. The land formation was intimidating, and looked as if it was straight out of the Jurassic period. The only thing missing from sight was dinosaurs, yet this jungle was so dense and untraveled by man, it wouldn't be hard for one's imagination to conjure the idea of such creatures lurking in the shadows.

For nearly an hour more, our journey led us slowly down the steep slippery sides of the ravine. Thick mud grabbed at our boots as exposed tree roots did everything in their power to trip us where the mud failed to slow our progress. The crew battled the environment constantly as we hauled camera gear and day supplies, all the while doing our very best to avoid the plethora of venomous animals hidden in silence beneath the leaves. Every step counted as a blessing, as the very next one could potentially be the last.

By the time the sun was directly overhead, we were just breaking trail onto the creek bed; we were exactly where we needed to be to pursue one of the rainforest's most elusive creatures; an animal whispered about in native lore that carried with it a haunting mystique and rumored dangers of a deadly touch. The legend was that if a human were to come in contact with it, even just grazing its skin, that certain doom would directly follow!

In your mind, I bet you are picturing some giant dinosaur-like lizard armed with claws and a forked tongue, or perhaps a bizarre looking creepy-crawly with massive fangs and a nightmarish stinger. I have some surprising news. The target of this epic journey is no bigger than the tip of a finger with a skeletal structure as fragile as glass, yet a defense so potent that it can kill even the most dangerous predator in the rainforest. This amphibian is often heard and very rarely seen. Its brilliant coloration of red and blue make it look like a piece of candy dropped from the pocket of a child, which would make one think it must be nearly impossible to miss, especially if you were inclined to search for it.

Have you guessed what this legendary creature might be?

I peered out into the flowing creek water, and just when it seemed as if all hope had been lost and the expedition would need to be chalked up as a failure, the rain miraculously began to let up and in just a matter of minutes came to a complete halt. That is the amazing thing about Costa Rica; one minute it's a downpour, the next it's a lush humid maze of saturated plants and mud.

My fingers were crossed as I stepped out and onto the creek bed. With hopeful hesitation, I peered up into the sky and saw the gray clouds breaking apart before my very eyes as a brilliant clear blue revealed itself and sharp rays of blinding sunlight cascaded down through the canopy.

"Guys, I think this is our window... the rain could return at any time, so let's spread out and begin searching the embankments for poison frogs!" I was excited! We had come so far, and our search for this elusive gem of the rainforest was finally about to begin; a search that would be like finding a jelly bean among muddy leaves and shadows.

Poison frogs can be incredibly difficult to catch despite their bright *aposematic coloration*, as they often have precise and calculated escape routes into burrows or log cavities that quickly protect them from a predator's attack.

'Wait, wait, wait... what was that big word you just used and what in the world does it mean!?'

Ah yes, *aposematic coloration*! That is a fancy word for warning colors. Most often when you encounter a terrestrial animal, be it an amphibian, reptile, or insect that has distinctive or elaborate coloration on its skin, scales, or spines, it is a warning that they are either venomous or poisonous.

'If you get too close, my bite can be deadly, and if you touch me or try to eat me, there is a good chance that I will be the last thing you ever feast upon!'

When it comes to poison frogs specifically, whether they are blue and red, green and black, yellow and orange, or any other bright combination, their coloration warning screams that they are seriously toxic. Some species are so toxic that even handling one can kill a human; however, most species are relatively harmless as long as they are not eaten. So, a word to the wise... never eat a poison frog!

The crew and I were clearly not interested in a poison frog lunch, but instead, hoped to get the granular poison frog up close for the cameras so that we could share this incredible little amphibian with the audience.

"So, Coyote, what are we looking for?" Mark called out from behind the lens.

"Well, Mark, it's not so much that we are looking as it is we are listening. The real key to locating one of these frogs is to first hear them calling. Males are constantly calling to the females, and if you can locate a frog with your ears, then it's just a matter of time before you can quietly follow the sound and hopefully make visual contact..."

My explanation was suddenly cut short as I heard the call of a poison frog from just a few yards away. Their call is very distinct, a shrill chirp, almost like a cricket call with a long draw to its end which then echoes into the next chirp as it quickly repeats for several cycles in a row.

With eyes open wide, I looked back and directly into the lens of the camera. This could be it! My obvious excitement beamed from the wide smile on my face as I silently held up a hand, pausing the camera crew's forward progress. We listened again. The rainforest was silent, aside from the droplets of water that fell from the leaves and plopped into the puddles on the creek bed floor. The sound echoed in slow repetitions as we patiently listened, ears perked and in tune with every passing second.

"Chiiiirrrrrrpppppppp, Chiiiirrrrrrrpppppppp, Chiiiiiirrrrrrpppppp!" the frog called again, and I quickly spun to my left and inched my way toward the underbrush. Massive leaves drooped, heavy with rain, and I carefully ducked beneath them so as not to disturb the environment. Just a single wrong move, sound, or splash of water could send a visible poison frog leaping for the safety of its burrow.

"I see him, I see him... Come up slow." I motioned for the crew to follow carefully and quietly behind me.

I took another step forward and arched my neck around the trunk of a small tree. THERE IT WAS! Perched with poise and dignity, the frog stood with his forearms locked in place and his chest puffed out. He called again, loud and proud. It was amazing to see and hear such a tiny creature making so mighty a sound. Clearly, he was the prince of his rainforest cathedral and he was telling his kingdom that he was in search of a mate. Only instead of drawing in a lucky lady frog... he had drawn in Coyote Peterson and the Brave Wilderness crew.

"Ok, this is it, our chance to actually catch a granular poison Frog that is just inches away, but it's going to take an incredible amount of care and precision. This is not an alligator, folks, it's not an arachnid with an armor-like exoskeleton; this is one of the most delicate amphibians on the planet, and it's tiny, no bigger than the nail of my thumb... and they are lightning quick. Are you ready for this?"

Mark nodded his head in silence as I sent a glance to Chance, who had perfectly positioned himself about 10 feet away and was stabilizing the camera on a fallen tree trunk, lens zoomed in and focus racked. From under the brim of his Brave Wilderness ball cap his eyes met mine and he nodded. It was go time.

My strategy was simple: get in front of the frog and with a little gentle coaxing try my best to get the amphibian to hop directly onto my hand. I am sure this sounds impossible, but you don't catch a poison frog like you would a bull frog or a cane toad. Due to its size and fragility, any contact I had needed to be incredibly gentle.

With cunning stealth, I slinked over the decomposing jungle floor and strategically positioned myself in front of the frog. Clearly it had noticed our presence, as the calling had ceased and the amphibian had lowered its position from upright and proud to hunched and hidden. Little did the frog know that because of its bright coloration – glistening ruby red and aquamarine skin in the moist rainforest air – it stuck out like a sore thumb on its green leafy perch. I looked down at the frog and took a final step toward it. Crouching down very slowly, I brought my knees to the forest floor, leaned forward, and extended my hand toward this pint-sized beauty.

The frog was likely thinking, "Go ahead, eat me! I dare you, predator... just see what happens if you decide that I am going to be your afternoon snack!"

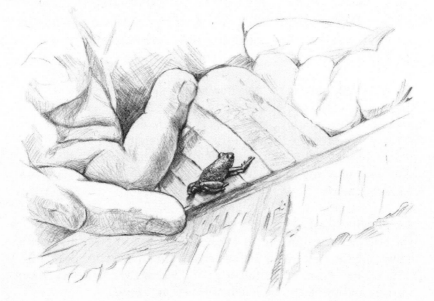

The good news for the frog was that the last thing on my mind was having an amphibian appetizer.

"Let me see if can just get him to hop up onto my hand..." I reached my other hand behind the frog and gently touched the back side of his hind legs; in an almost mechanical burst he hopped forward and straight onto my outstretched hand. "There we go, got him. Awesome!" I quickly cupped the frog and turned back toward the camera. "Now that we finally got one, let's get out into the better light and get him up close to the cameras."

In an excited scramble, Mark and Chance worked the cameras out from beneath the underbrush, and we spilled out onto the creek bed. The smile on Mario's face told me that he was beyond thrilled, and he called out as I hurried up ahead of the cameras, "You good, Coyote? You know everything you want to talk about with this little guy?" As our wildlife biologist, Mario always does his best to make sure that I am on point with my facts and that everyone is safe when we are interacting with an animal. I was incredibly confident with my facts when it came to the granular poison frog, and despite it being toxic, I had very little fear when it came to interacting with it.

I hollered back in Mario's direction and assured him I was ready to present the scene. "Yeah buddy, I'm good to go... Man, we did it – a true jewel of the rainforest!"

I could not wait to talk about this frog! We had finally managed to find and catch what I considered to be one of the most elegant amphibians in Central America.

Once the cameras were set and rolling I immediately began to present the facts: "One of the most interesting things about the granular variety that sets them apart from many other poison frog species is the 'granulated' nature of their skin. Imagine little grains of sand beneath the slimy surface of an amphibian's skin, and you can picture what the texture of this frog is like. In a way, it almost looks like a toad, yet it is indeed a frog." Its bright red body was incredibly striking, like a ruby glistening in the beams of sunlight cast sharply though the tree canopy, and as I directed the camera lens to follow my finger down the length of its body, the aquamarine coloration of its belly and hind legs came into view.

This animal was incredible; its patterning was perfectly displayed as an aposematic warning to potential predators. I gently held the animal on the tip of my finger, balancing it with care and precision, as a frog of this size is incredibly fragile. With a pure sense of fascination and amazement, I began to warn the audience about the poison frog's toxicity:

"I'm pretty safe right now. I'm sure you're all watching this thinking to yourselves, 'Oh boy, Coyote, here you go again, handling another dangerous animal.' Trust me, I'm in no danger as long as I don't lick or eat this little tiny frog." I continued by explaining the frog's defensive bright coloration, which warns predators of its toxicity. "This specific species is not quite as toxic as some others. There are some species in South America that are so potent that if they so much as touch human skin, they can kill a full-grown man in a matter of hours!"

I carefully spun the frog in a semicircle to give the cameras a head-on look at the frog's face and its very distinct black beady eyes. "The eyes of these frogs are very large in comparison to their heads, which provides them with excellent sight when they are out hunting in the shadows of the rainforest floor."

"The diet of a poison frog varies, and they are considered opportunistic predators, but their primary target is usually small invertebrates like ants and mites, which help provide the frog with the necessary alkaloids to produce the toxin that is in their skin. This makes poison frogs rather unique, in that the food that provides them nutrients also helps to keep them protected from becoming food themselves!"

It's not every day that you can work with an animal as small and innocent-looking as this one and make such a statement. So while catching the animal wasn't the most dramatic encounter we have managed to get on camera, the unique, almost superhero, aspects of the animal itself really made it an episode worth filming.

Next, we took care in examining the frog's front and back feet, noting that unlike many species of frogs, their toes are not webbed. With an inquisitive nature, I asked Mark, "Do you know why that is?"

His reply was the perfect setup for my next fact. "Is it because they don't actually live in water like other frogs?"

I quickly jumped back into the conversation, "That's right, poison frogs are terrestrial, which means that they live their existence primarily on land. Now, they do occasionally visit the water for breeding purposes; however, most of their time is spent climbing through the leaf litter, over logs, and even occasionally up the side of a tree to forage for food. Their homes are often made in elaborate root structures or in burrows on the sides of valley walls, exactly like the area we have been exploring today."

Mark interjected, "So that's the reason we're on this epic expedition!"

"EXACTLY! Sometimes you really have to push the limits to get close to animals like this. A granular poison frog can't be found just anywhere in the rainforest. They live a very calculated existence and rely heavily on certain aspects of the terrain for their very survival. Nonetheless, it was absolutely worth the effort of the long arduous hike and all that torrential rain to ultimately get this frog up close to the cameras!"

I was nearing the end of my presentation, and I could clearly tell it was time to return this delicate amphibian to the wild. When we work with amphibians, we can't spend too much time filming the scene, as handling them quickly absorbs the necessary moisture from their skin. So as much as we wished to stay and spend the afternoon with this handsome little creature, we knew that the scene needed to be wrapped up quickly.

In the background Mario quietly removed a small notebook from his pocket, fanned through the pages, and ran down his list of facts with a steady finger. Everything seemed covered; this was almost a wrap. Only one last thing to do...

With my face close to the frog, I looked into those black beady eyes; entranced by its returned gaze, we shared a moment. From my perspective, I felt a certain respect for this tiny yet fragile amphibian, who was toxic enough to keep itself alive up against even the most feared predators of the rainforest.

In my mind, I hoped that the frog looked back at me and thought to itself, "Cool. This guy didn't try to eat me, he just talked about me and admired my awesomeness! Not that bad for an encounter of the human kind!"

Whenever we work with potentially dangerous animals, I always feel that it is important to remind the audience of the possible hazards and risks of doing so, and I make it a point to address this on camera.

"Even though the toxins in the granular poison frog are not potent enough to harm me from just handling it, I definitely want to wash my hands with soap and water as soon as possible. If you ever happen upon one of these frogs in the wild, keep in mind that besides being toxic, they are also unbelievably fragile, so it's always best to just admire them from a safe distance, ensuring a great encounter for the both of you."

After I delivered my coined outro, "Be Brave, Stay Wild...we'll see you on the next adventure!" we carefully moved the frog back into the underbrush so that we could release it in the exact same place we found it.

With cupped hands, I knelt down and slowly opened up my fingers, revealing the frog for the cameras. Warm rainforest air blanketed my outstretched hands, and in that very moment the frog felt freedom, it sprang from my palms and back into the maze of forest floor underbrush. The leap was so fast, it was almost as if the frog disappeared into thin air. I looked back at the cameras in amazement, since I didn't think any of us could believe how fast the animal disappeared.

With a sigh of relief, I gazed up into the tree canopy above me as white beams of sunlight cascaded down and warmed my face. This truly was an expedition that had seemed impossible; one that had pushed us to the limit, causing us to question whether we could pull it off and find, let alone catch, a poison frog.

Looking back, I will never forget that moment where my body was soaked in water and mud, and I felt exhausted to the core and fraught with discouragement from the environmental challenges we faced. In that moment, although we thought about quitting,

we pressed onward, as we have done time and time again... and somehow we managed to prevail.

I high-fived the crew in excitement – we all knew that we had one incredible episode in the can.

The towering valley walls surrounded us with a reminder that the hike back to base camp was going to be just as difficult as the trip in. With a first step toward home, our boots began to splash back up the creek, and I knew in my heart that today, nature had truly given us a treasure more valuable than gold.

They say that good things come in small packages, but when it comes to the granular poison frog, a true gem of the Osa Peninsula rainforest, it's probably more accurate to say that dangerous things come in small packages, too!

Chapter 7

BEAR SCARE!

L et's face it, we all have fears. While we all have fears unique to our experiences in life, the fact remains that inside all of us is something we're afraid of, and to admit these fears is not a sign of weakness. In fact, fear is a healthy part of everyday life, as it often helps guide us around potential dangers that seem to be ever present and ready to pop up at a moment's notice. Being brave has nothing to do with being fearless and everything to do with how we face fear itself.

In my journeys, I have broken trail and traversed rugged terrain in many remote areas; however, no place has ever been wilder or more intimidating than the great state of Alaska. Described as the last frontier, Alaska is BIG, bigger than anything I had ever seen. The first moment I stepped foot in the town of Haines, looking around at the towering mountain ranges, I knew instantly this was going to be the adventure of a lifetime.

The mountains were sculpted by the long, harsh Northern winters and capped with pure white snow. Below the snow line, the dark slate-colored rock eventually gave way to evergreen forests that were dense, dark, and ancient. Enormous trees towered into the sky, wrapped in gnarled bark and curtains of hanging moss. These forests were the kind of place where one could walk just a few feet in and become lost in a maze of shadows.

Deep within the mountain valleys and hidden amongst the forest shadows, this 660,000 square acre expanse is home to some of the planet's most iconic animal species, many of which are almost impossible to see unless you are lucky enough to be in the right place at the perfect moment. Even then, you may only catch a glimpse of fur or a flash of feathers, as the animals of Alaska often do an incredible job at staying hidden from the eyes of man.

Having an animal encounter in an environment like this usually begins with knowing exactly where to look.

Direct your eyes to the sky, and you may see the vast wingspan of a bald eagle, a true American icon with its elegant white head and matching tail. Their feathers glisten in the sun as they soar through the clouds and hunt with their incredible binocular vision, scanning the frigid rushing rivers below. If you gaze beneath the surface of the flowing water, you may see hundreds of sockeye salmon rushing up river. If these speedy fish manage to avoid the talons of an eagle on the hunt, they will return to the same spawning grounds where they were born and will complete their lifecycle as they reproduce, die, and return to the earth.

Between the sky and the water live a plethora of animals that call the open fields, silt flats, forests, and mountainsides their home. Many of them are mammals, ranging from tiny predators like the Short-

tailed weasel to its larger, more famously ferocious cousin, the wolverine. Then there are the pack hunters like gray wolves and coyotes, as well as stealthy felines such as lynx, bobcats, and mountain lions. The carnivores are constantly on the hunt, yet their herbivore counterparts, the moose, caribou, and bison spend their days roaming the craggy terrain foraging for plants.

The list goes on and on, as Alaska is home to over 100 species of mammals, but not a single one is more iconic than the one you are probably thinking we forgot to mention... the brown bear.

If there is one animal that can be named the undisputed predatory heavyweight champion of the Alaskan wilderness, the title definitely belongs to the brown bear. A fully grown male can tip the scales at nearly 1,500 pounds, reach speeds of nearly 30 mph, and are considered by many to be the most dangerous animal one can encounter while hiking in the wild. No one ever expects to be attacked by a bear, yet attacks do occasionally happen. It might be surprising, but happening upon a mother and her cubs is actually more dangerous than coming face to face with a rogue male. These tragic moments often occur when a hiker stumbles upon and spooks a protective mother, triggering her deep instinctual nature to defend her offspring.

I am sure this sounds terrifying, but if everyone in Alaska, whether resident or visitor, spent their lives worrying about bear attacks, no one would ever get outside to enjoy its beauty. Sources say that there is roughly one brown bear for every 21 residents in the frontier state; luckily there are many precautions one can take to avoid an attack. However, if an attack becomes unavoidable, there are a few key decisions you can make that have the potential to diffuse the situation so everyone walks away unscathed.

The following encounter happened to me in the summer of 2016, and to this day still sends chills down my spine whenever I tell it.

As the sun slowly sank in the sky, moving toward the crest of the mountains, a strong breeze rushed through the valley and whipped off the surface of the river. Taking a deep breath, I inhaled the pure smell of the cool Alaskan air. Fresh and sweet, it danced into my nose and glazed my senses with a hint of pine before filling my lungs. I absorbed the moment and wondered to myself, 'is this exactly what it smelled like during the start of the gold rush in the late 1800's?'

It must have been. Oh, the incredible sense of adventure a man would have felt being one of the first to explore this land, facing its perils while searching for a stake in the mountainside that would lead to vast riches! I was lost in my fantasy, envisioning myself 120 years ago: dressed in a cowboy hat, rifle strung over my shoulder, and leading a pack horse across the silt flats; my hands weathered and worn as they clutched the reins, eyes bright with wondrous hope, and a burly beard growing grizzly upon my face; a man in a new land with a dream to make a name for myself by braving the wild to find and lay claim to the treasure of a lifetime.

My daydream was suddenly interrupted by a crisp chill on my leg and the realization that the river was seeping over the brim of my worn hiking boots. I looked down as they pressed into the charcoal-colored silt, creating suction that temporarily glued me in place, allowing the flowing water to soak me.

"Awww... great!" I thought sarcastically as I struggled to get free, looking anything but graceful as I nearly toppled over into the water trying to escape.

Mark, who watched this moment of elegance from a short distance away, called out in my direction to get a status update on my current predicament:

"Hey man, you good? You need some help?"

The saturated silt flats were like quicksand, and if you stood in one place too long they would attempt to swallow you alive. I wasn't going to succumb to mere mud, and I confidently clapped back. "Oh yeah, I'm good, man. Don't worry about me!"

Finally, I pulled my now soaked and silt-covered boots up from the mud and climbed onto a log. Looking down at my feet, it appeared as if I had dipped my lower limbs into a tar-like cake batter. It was nearly impossible to recognize that the massive globs at the ends of my legs were even boots. I kicked my feet, flinging thick silt mud into the air as Mark updated me on his plan for filming the setting sun.

"Mario and I are going to head up river a bit and try to get some shots of the sun as it disappears behind that mountain peak.

The light looks really epic, and the reflections off the river could make some great location photography for the wolverine episode!"

I signaled him with a thumbs-up, as I was confident that he and Mario would get some amazing shots, plus I needed to get my feet into the flowing water to remedy this muddy situation.

"You guys have bear spray, right!?" I hollered out as they began to head up river. Mario turned back toward me and held up a red can wrapped in a black holster and nodded his head.

That's right, bear spray; a deterrent similar to self-defense pepper spray but much more potent. If deployed in the direction of a charging bear, the spray creates a plume of peppery pain that will irritate the animal's eyes, nose, and mouth. In theory, this irritation will stop a bear's forward momentum, sending the attacking predator fleeing in the opposite direction and giving you the chance to quickly make an escape. They say bear spray is the one thing you must always take into bear country, and trust me when I say that the entire state of Alaska is an endless maze of bear country.

For days, we had been roaming the wilderness filming episodes and had seen many traces of these lumbering nomadic giants. From scat (more commonly known as bear poop) to track ways along the river's edge and even the remains of half-consumed salmon carcasses, we were surrounded by reminders that the bears were here, even if we had yet to actually see one.

With my own canister of bear spray secured snugly yet easily accessible at my hip, I turned away from Mark and Mario and called out to our photographer, Austin, who was snapping shots of some fresh bear tracks along the water's edge.

If you can't set your camera's sights on a bear, you may as well capture their tracks, and they sure were impressive. It's a strange feeling to be in the wild and know you are in the ever-looming presence of bears. The tracks Austin was photographing were fresh, incredibly fresh, perhaps no more than 30 minutes old; and they were concrete evidence that even though it seemed as if we were alone out on this river, we truly were not.

Bear tracks are incredible. If you have ever seen them in the wild, then you know what I mean. The weight of a 1,000 pound animal pressing down into soft silt creates these perfect impressions where the heel pads have sunk in, and the claws, about an inch in front of the toe pads, cut into the ground, leaving a haunting reminder that these animals command lethal power. Their front paws are armed with five razor-sharp claws, which are used to dig, to defend, or to disembowel prey. Just a single swipe of a bear's front paw to the face, neck, or chest of a human can easily take their life.

I bent down and placed my hand next to the track so that Austin could use it as reference for a photo. The print dwarfed my hand; it made the hairs on the back of my neck stand on end. I could almost feel the energy of this animal, and I pictured it in my mind slowly traveling up river, following its nose to the pockets of salmon that would certainly be at the top of the list on this evening's dinner menu. I looked up toward Austin and expressed my awe.

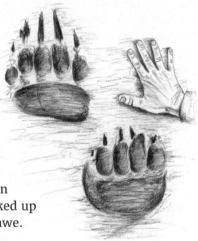

"Wow, that's a big bear, definitely a male, and it looks like he may have been here as little as a half hour ago. We probably want to do everything in our power to avoid him, so let's head down river a bit and see if we can find any skulls or bones that may have gotten washed into those log snags."

Searching for antler sheds and animal bones has always been my form of treasure hunting, and Austin loved the game just as much as I did. So, with eyes fixated on the river's edge, along the embankments, and constantly scanning the twists and tangles of the log snags, we made our way downriver.

The water system was flowing with incredible speed, as it cut like a network of veins in several directions down and across the silt flats. The sound was hypnotizing; a constant low drone of water rushing over rocks that overwhelmed our hearing as we continued our search. It was a walk to remember as this land was timeless, virtually untouched by man and quite possibly the wildest place I had ever set foot.

I stood on the edge of the river, studying my surroundings, taking in the magnificence of our present setting. The light was beautiful the way it illuminated the low hanging clouds, and together they painted the evening sky like an artist's flowing brush strokes. I felt lost in beauty and I just couldn't believe how epic this northern state truly was.

I looked at the watch on my wrist, realizing it was nearly eight o'clock in the evening and we had yet to come across any antlers or remains; not even a single rib or femur bone. Sadly, it looked as if our treasure hunt was coming to a close for the day. We started heading toward Mark and Mario so we could return to our cabins at Mosquito Lake and rest up for the next day's filming.

As we walked, Austin and I talked about our love of photography, a conversation that had us more focused on cameras and technology than it did our surroundings. This was our biggest mistake, and it highlights a lesson I always try to stress to anyone who is watching or listening to our Brave Wilderness content. Always, and I mean ALWAYS, pay attention to your surroundings, especially in Alaska.

Heading upriver, the wind was in our face, meaning that anything ahead of us would not be able to catch our scent as we walked westward toward the blinding setting sun. The sound of the flowing water to our right was deafening, and we were shouting just to converse at the distance of only a couple feet. I make mention of these environmental factors because the combination of wind, light, and sound are always being used by animals to cleverly avoid humans.

With its extremely sensitive nose, the brown bear can smell animals and humans, alive or dead, from miles away if the wind is blowing in their direction. They can also hear footsteps approaching from several hundred yards, giving them ample time to duck into the underbrush to avoid any unwanted interaction with a potential hunter. Their vision, however, with their small, beady eyes is rather poor, which is why they rely so heavily on their senses of smell and hearing.

In a downwind, low light scenario, like the one Austin and I found ourselves in, a bear would not be able to smell or physically see us coming until we were dangerously close, and the sounds of the rushing river meant a bear would not hear us either.

Little did we know it at the time, but Austin and I were in the midst of a perfect storm. All three natural elements, wind, water, and light, were not only working against us, but also against the powerful senses of any approaching predator; and unknown to us, one was only about 200 yards away.

The next few moments felt as if they played out in slow motion. I had walked several yards ahead of Austin and was looking down at my feet as I balanced on the river's edge. Suddenly, I had a very strange feeling – a sense of unease blanketed my entire body. Instinctually, I stopped dead in my tracks and slowly lifted my head. The sunlight glistened sharply in my eyes, and suddenly the collision course we were on revealed itself, no more than 150 yards in front of us.

Amid the stark beams of light and hazy shadows, a massive brown bear materialized from behind a cluster of dense brambles. It was a moment I will never forget, an image that will never be erased from my mind, and a feeling I hope never to experience again.

My heart dropped like a ton of rocks and landed in my stomach

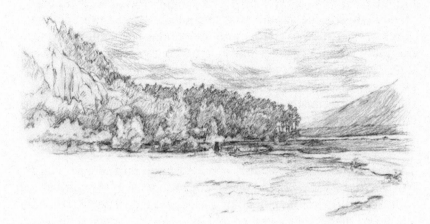

with a crash. With a trembling and inexperienced hand, I quickly reached for and fumbled with the bear spray on my hip. Finally yanking it from the nylon holster, I looked down in panic as I scrambled to pull the safety pin. While doing so, I forced out the only words I could muster... the only word on my mind, the only thing I could see as the visual expanse before me zoomed in on the massive animal that was lumbering straight toward us.

"Bear! Bear! Austin, BEAR!" I shouted and he stopped dead in his tracks, frozen mid-stride now just a few feet behind me.

Nearly 1,000 pounds of muscle and bulk were coming straight toward us, and it was clear that the bear did not see, smell, or hear us. My heart was racing, and all I could think was, "When do I deploy the bear spray, because this bear is close enough to charge and attack!"

Just as I had that thought, the scenario took an incredible turn for the worse. From beyond the underbrush three cubs appeared, seemingly out of thin air. This bear was a she-bear, a sow, a mama bear... WITH CUBS! This was the most dangerous scenario we could ever find ourselves in with bears, and they were now closing in at a distance of 100 yards.

I instructed Austin to stay behind me as I readied the bear spray.

Anticipating a charge was my first thought, and I needed to be ready to deploy the blinding peppery substance in the animal's direction if it showed aggression. My hand was shaking holding the spray in front of me, while clutched in my other hand was a GoPro camera on a steady mount. Since I am also a filmmaker at heart, my immediate thought after preparing the bear spray was to turn on the camera and start recording. If this was to be my last animal encounter, I was at least going to go down getting it all on camera!

The mother and her cubs were about to climb up and over a large cluster of snarled trees and debris that had washed down river and collected on the raised embankment. It was a do-or-die moment, as I knew that if they came up and over the tree snags there would be less than 75 yards between us. This proximity would increase the likelihood of her being startled upon spotting us, which could ultimately lead to a charge and a greater chance of an attack. Remember, at full sprint, brown bears can reach speeds of nearly 30 mph and can cover 100 yards in a matter of seconds. So, I made one of the most important and risky, yet calculated, decisions I have ever made in my life. It was time. I had to alert the bears of our presence.

I braced myself, one hand clenched around the bear spray hoping it wouldn't be necessary, my other hand shaking as I did my best to keep the camera steady. I took a deep breath and then let out a call to the bear – the most basic call possible, but a tactic they often teach in wilderness survival training.

"HEY, BEAR! HEY, BEAR!" I hollered as loud as I could, but the sound of the river and wind deadened my alert calls. She couldn't hear me, and all four bears were still coming straight toward us. Panic was setting in, and I called again. This time Austin joined in to create the loudest alert possible.

"HEY, BEARS, YO BEARS... BACK UP, BEAR!" Austin began waving his hands in the air to create a visual signal and line of sight for the approaching animals.

"YO BEAR, HEY, BEAR, BACK UP, BEAR!" we continued to holler as loud as we could; suddenly, one of the cubs heard us and spotted us. It stopped still with its ears perked up and its body language on immediate alarm, which in turn signaled its siblings to take notice of the source of the panic. Almost in unison they went on alert; one even stood up on its hind legs, while the others looked left and right. We screamed again, as the mother was still steadily advancing toward us.

"GET BACK, BEARS! GET BACK, BEAR!"

Finally, the mother saw us. One of the most terrifying moments in my life was the moment when this enormous mother Brown Bear turned her head and looked straight at us. Her snout lifted and her lips relaxed as she snorted and sniffed the air with her black shiny nose. She still hadn't quite seen us, but at this juncture she most definitely had heard us and had given the cubs the high alert signal.

Displaying her sheer strength, she pushed off from the soft river's edge with her massive front paws and raised herself up to her hind legs. She was magnificent, intimidating, and absolutely mammoth in size. From her upright height, she could see over the log snags, and without a doubt, she saw us. The mother bear towered over her cubs.

The top of her head easily reached close to seven feet in the air, and we estimated a weight of around 800 pounds... an enormous animal. She was either going to rally her cubs and flee in the opposite direction toward the safety of the underbrush, or she was going to charge us and defend them violently with bone-crushing jaws and razor-sharp claws.

There was no question that the cubs were about to take action. They looked panicked and began to pace back and forth. We had no idea what the mother was going to do. Time slowed down; what felt like minutes couldn't have been more than a few seconds. At that moment, our calls fell silent. My hand was shaking... I had the bear spray aimed and ready, yet I had no idea at what distance to deploy the peppery deterrent. All I could think about was standing my ground, telling myself that no matter what, even if she charges... DO NOT RUN!

Austin, being the complete maniac that he is, for some reason thought it would be a great time to lift up his camera and begin snapping photos! Click, click, click, click. I could hear the shutter firing off shot after shot, a sound I will never forget, as those could have quite possibly been the last shots he would ever take if this bear decided she needed to defend her cubs from the potential threat.

The seconds drew out like hours, my eyes glued to the bear, and I watched as the breeze lifted her golden-brown coat into the air. She was beautiful, a perfect specimen of her species. The kind of bear you see painted in the pictures of a book. The queen of the north stood before us, and our survival hinged on her next decision.

I remember my mind whispering, 'Please turn around, please turn around', and it was almost in that exact instant that she exhaled. I could see the animal's powerful breath pluming over her lips from her long snout. She made her decision and dropped to all fours with a staggering impact, and then whoosh... she swung her head to the right and turned away from us. The three cubs followed suit, and as a family unit they bolted at an incredible pace back in the opposite direction. Just as quickly as they had appeared on the river's edge, they disappeared into a cloud of dust that rose up and caught the breeze, where it drifted off down river and into the waning golden sunlight.

Austin turned toward me and we locked eyes. We were speechless. Standing still for several moments, we held our ground, since we wanted to make sure the bears were clear of the area. It has been recorded that a mother will move her cubs away from danger and then return to the scene of encounter to attack the threat. This moment was incredibly nerve-wracking, so we continued to make lots of loud noise, clapping, hollering, and shouting for Mark and Mario.

After nearly five minutes, we were fairly certain the bears were gone, and we approached the log snags. Carefully we climbed up and over, descending to the soft river bank below, where we discovered a beautiful cluster of tracks; perfect impressions in the damp silt. I continued to film the experience as Austin honed in

on the mother bear's tracks, specifically the front paws where she had landed from her upright stance. The size and strength of the animal were made apparent by the intimidating impressions left by her pads and claws.

Shouts from the distance could be heard as Mark and Mario returned.

"Coyote, Austin... where are you guys?!" Mark called out.

I answered, "OVER HERE, RIVER'S EDGE, KEEP HEADING DOWN RIVER!"

As they returned, Mark powered on his camera, as he and Mario had heard and witnessed the entire event. He began filming a candid on-location moment between all four of us. The energy was high; the danger had been as real as anything we had ever experienced. As a team, we were writhing with excitement, adrenaline, and utter disbelief at what had just happened. The looming threat of the mother returning, while unlikely, was still possible, so after a few more photos of the tracks, we cut cameras and quickly moved in the direction of our vehicle.

The brown bear is one of the most powerful land mammals in North America, and they should always be revered and respected. Bear attacks are rare; in most cases a bear will do everything in its power to avoid human interaction. However, if you do have an encounter, there are a few basic decisions you can make and some simple actions you can take that may save your life.

If you stumble upon a brown bear in the wild and it does NOT see you, and you have the ability to quietly and quickly move off in the opposite direction, DO SO. If you and the bear make visual contact with one another, and the animal begins to advance toward you... holler, scream, wave your arms in the air and make yourself look as large, scary, and crazy as possible. In almost every reported case of an encounter where a human has attempted to scare off a bear, it has worked.

Seeing a bear in the wild is both exciting and terrifying, especially if you are in close proximity to the animal. One of the most important things you need to remember is that no matter what, never, and I mean NEVER, run. If you do, it will likely trigger the bear's predatory instinct to target you and chase you down. Despite anything you may have previously heard or read, humans cannot outrun bears. Ever.

If a brown bear charges, and you are hiking with bear spray, deploy the spray when the bear is closing on your location at 25 yards. The plume of peppery mist will fill its eyes, nasal cavity, and mouth, causing extreme discomfort and confusion. If you are lucky, this will be enough to send the bear running in the opposite direction, or possibly buy you enough time to escape up a tree or onto a nearby boulder. If you cannot deploy the spray, cannot escape, and an attack is inevitable, never try to fight the bear, you will not win. Your best chance for survival is dropping to the ground, curling your body into a ball, clutching your hands tightly over the back of your head and neck, and holding on... because it's going to be bad. But a brown bear wants to eliminate the threat, not necessarily eat you. So if it thinks you are dead, you might just possibly escape with your life.

There is arguably no greater land predator in North America than the brown bear. Their lumbering, confident stride clearly exemplifies their place at the top of the food chain. Seeing one of these magnificent animals in its natural setting is something I will never forget. Being in a scenario where I was forced to use my wilderness survival skills for a bear encounter was exciting. But I am the first to admit when I am afraid, and on that evening along the river's edge, I was truly afraid, not only for my own life, but for the life of my friend Austin.

I remember returning to the truck, opening the door, climbing inside, and slamming it shut behind me. Within the protective confines of the metal and glass of the truck, my heart was still racing. The engine turned over, the gas was punched, and we headed down the old logging road toward camp. No one said a word; we rode silently to the sound of tires bouncing through potholes, and the dust in the wake of our vehicle was the only thing left behind.

I don't know what was going through Austin's mind, and I don't know what Mark and Mario were thinking about, but I am pretty sure their thoughts were similar to mine. We had just encountered a mother brown bear and her three cubs, one of the most dangerous scenarios you can ever encounter in nature, and we all walked away without a scratch.

With glassy eyes, I peered out the window as remnants of the setting sun cast a lingering glow in the never-darkening Alaskan summer sky. As we distanced ourselves from the site of the encounter, I could feel my heart rate finally begin to calm, and a sense of relief set in. At last, I felt safe.

This "bear scare" is a tale that I will tell for the rest of my life, and it provided me with a crystal-clear realization: No matter how confident I am in my abilities, as a human in the wild, I'm not the one in control. I will always be at the mercy of the elements and the animals that call the location home. It is a statement of truth and an expression of honesty to say that even I am faced with moments of real fear. Yet in the aftermath of it all, I do not see this fear as a weakness, but rather as a well-earned sense of respect for the heavyweight champion of the north, and the true ruler of the Alaskan frontier... the brown bear.

Chapter 8

Swimming with Giants!

A s someone who has grown up with incredible love and respect for all the creatures that call our planet home, my goal with every wildlife encounter is to hopefully make a true and lasting connection. These moments, when caught on camera, become videos on the Brave Wilderness channel, allowing people from across the world to live vicariously through my experiences. Every interaction is different, and I never know when the connection will occur. Occasionally I am left feeling unsatisfied, as if I have somehow missed my opportunity to make a positive impression.

However, there are many encounters I have had in which I do feel a strong bond was formed. I can look back on them with fondness, as these are the moments in my life of adventure that I will never forget. It's hard to pick a single favorite, but if you were to ask me which connection was the most heartwarming, it would without question be the one where I swam with giants.

An eerie morning fog sat above the water as our boat slowly motored up Crystal River. The light creeping in from the horizon was reflected on its mirror–like calm surface. I watched as the bow broke the light to pieces, scattering it on the waves that rolled off in our wake. The sun was still several minutes away from rising in the eastern sky, and as I stood on the deck, my body shivered in the crisp morning air. It was early December on the gulf coast of Florida, and while the days were warm with sunshine and blue skies, the winter nights and mornings brought significant cold spells with them. This morning was especially frigid.

Warmly tucked in the heated cabin, our captain signaled my attention, knocking on the window and pointing with his thumb. I looked off to the starboard side of the boat and perched in the trees along the embankment, my eyes beheld hundreds of sleeping birds. Egrets, cormorants, and brown pelicans were all huddled together, awaiting the coming of the sun so that they could begin their morning fishing.

Excitement coursed through my body. This was going to be our first underwater episode of *Breaking Trail*, and as I looked back into the cabin, I watched Mark and Mario preparing the underwater housings for their cameras. We knew filming this episode would be a challenge, but if we could somehow pull it off, there was a good chance it would be epic.

We rounded a bend in the canal; it emptied out into a larger body of water known as Kings Bay, a protected wildlife sanctuary that is home to many animal species, but none more famous and adored than the Florida manatee. These gentle giants return in a massive migration to this area each winter to enjoy the consistently warm 72-degree Fahrenheit water temperatures. This warm bath of constantly flowing spring water is essential to the manatees' survival, as they are very susceptible to cold and cannot survive for extended periods of time in water that falls below 68 degrees. This migratory phenomenon fills the bay with hundreds of these enormous mammals between late November and early February, and upon first sight, it can be incredibly intimidating.

Like submarines, they rose from the darkness, their massive backs breaking the water's surface followed by their wrinkled noses, which blasted an exhalation of breath into the air, sending water spraying into the half-light of dawn. It was incredible the way their hefty bodies moved with such fluidity and grace as their large, round, flattened tails came to the surface. Then, in the blink of an eye, they would effortlessly descend and disappear into the dark watery abyss.

Poof! As quickly as the beasts had surfaced, they were gone.

The fog was finally beginning to burn off as the sharp beams of the rising sun scattered across the water's surface, revealing a minefield of breaching creatures. The manatees were awake, and knowing that these slow-moving animals were peaceful beings sent a wave of relief through me, supporting my anxious eagerness to enter the water.

My mind traveled back to the year 1513, and I envisioned myself as an early pioneering explorer like Ponce de Leon. He stumbled upon this panhandle state in his quest to find the "Fountain of Youth" and while that quest may have failed, he ultimately claimed this vast expanse of land for Spain. Five hundred years later, here I was, standing on the bow of a ship and looking out upon the same misty waters that were now home to descendants of the same creatures he must have witnessed. How terrifying it must have been to encounter an unknown monster of the deep, and not just one, but literally hundreds of them!

I don't know who the first person was to get into the water with a manatee, but the good news for them (and soon me) was that this animal is one of the gentlest creatures on the planet. Still, my heart was racing, with less than five minutes to our first dive with these majestic animals. With his camera rolling, Mario approached me to make sure I was ready to lead the crew into the manatee herd and get face-to-face with what are often referred to as "Sea Cows".

"You ready for your first contact with the Florida manatee, a real-life sea cow!"? he asked with a smile on his face. Since he was from Florida, Mario was no stranger to manatee encounters and had swum with them several times; however, today was a first for myself and Mark.

"As ready as I am ever going to be – but these flippers are kind of awkward!" I lifted my left foot while trying to balance on my right to display the large plastic fins that had replaced my normal hiking boots. In the process, I lost my balance, awkwardly grasped hold of the railing, and somehow managed to catch myself, preventing a fall from the boat and into the water. Whoo... that was a close one!

It's fair to say that on this expedition, I was truly a fish out of water. My normal adventure attire usually consists of a leather cowboy hat, button down shirt, backpack, hip pack, rugged cargo pants, and weathered hiking boots. Yet today my feet were housed in plastic flippers, my body encased in a skintight neoprene wetsuit, and my hat had been traded in for a mask and snorkel. I looked like a character from *20,000 Leagues Under the Sea*, but I

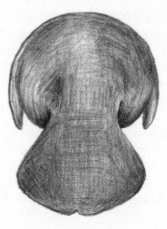

knew that my seal suit was going to be the best outfit for agility and speed when it came to maneuvering alongside a sea cow!

Our cameras were housed in these elaborate underwater contraptions that would protect them from the salt water as we submerged ourselves beneath the surface to get the shots we needed. Mark finished triple-checking the housings; gaskets all in place, screws tightened down, and clasps snapped closed. He exited the cabin and stood alongside Mario. With a mask over his eyes and the snorkel already gripped in his mouth he gave me a thumbs-up. It was time to go.

Mario handed me his camera, reached for his mask, and positioned it snugly over his eyes; with a thumbs-up, he too was ready. Now the show was just waiting on me to deliver my final lines from above the surface before we set off into the watery unknown, filled with thousand-pound swimming mammals.

7:43 a.m., time to enter the water!

"All right, we have manatees surrounding the boat right now. I'm trying to be as quiet as possible – we don't want to disturb them. This is the moment of truth, I am diving in – with the Manatees!"

Those were my last words to the camera before I cautiously climbed down the boat's port side ladder and slinked stealthily into the water, trying my best not to splash or create a wave that could startle the nearby animals. My heart was speeding at full throttle as the water permeated my wet suit and sent chills down my spine. The weight of the water pressed on my chest as I inhaled my first underwater breath. Even with the snorkel stack above the waterline, I still felt cautious about breathing with my face submerged; an uneasy feeling you may be familiar with if you have ever been snorkeling.

After a few careful breaths, I felt my heart rate begin to even out. 'I'm not inhaling water, I'm not drowning, I am snorkeling... This is awesome!' It took my brain a second to realize that I needed to look around me and absorb this view of the world from an underwater perspective.

It was aquamarine in color, mysterious in design, and haunting down there, the way sounds were completely muted and echoed in the recesses of my mind. My body felt weightless in the salty estuary water, and the wetsuit provided additional buoyancy. I realized that my legs were not moving, and I slowly began to kick them in a fluid rhythm to activate the abilities of my new fins in this moment of discovery. With surprising ease my body was propelled forward and away from the boat. It was incredible. I was swimming in a way I never had before.

From the corner of my dive mask I could see Mark and Mario, though it was tough to tell who was who in their matching suits. They looked more like space invaders than humans. Their bodies moved in unison to stay side by side as they held onto their underwater cameras. They signaled to me with a spinning motion, which I assumed meant to turn around. Just as I did, I made my first creature sighting beneath the surface. There are no words that can truly describe what it feels like to be in the presence of a manatee, floating with it in its own environment.

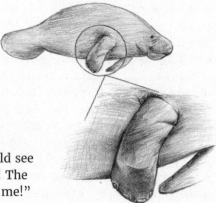

Through the murky water, I could see a dark shape, "Oh boy, this is it! The creature is coming right toward me!" I thought to myself.

My heart started to race again. In my mind, I understood that these animals were extremely kind and gentle, yet as the dark massive shape grew closer, it was hard to fight my instinct to be nervous. The animal was incredible the way it so effortlessly moved through the water. When it was no more than 10 feet from me, the manatee rolled onto its side just like a puppy and drifted with grace right past me.

Its blunted snout was slightly curved under and peppered with short coarse whiskers, perfectly designed for munching plants from the ocean floor. Its robust body was painted with wrinkles like the skin of an elephant, and its front flippers were tucked tightly against its chest. They were inviting, the way you remember your grandmother's hands being, and I just wanted to reach out and hold one... but I resisted and continued to admire the animal from a close distance.

The manatee completed its spin, revealing its rounded tail, which like a powerful paddle moved up, then down, propelling its body forward with a burst. From behind my mask, I watched in wonder as the massive shape which just seconds ago had grown into existence before my very eyes, now disappeared back into the fractals of light cutting like needles though the displaced water the animal left in its wake.

I had just experienced my first manatee encounter, and my heart was full of joy!

Like a kid who had gotten everything he asked for on Christmas morning and then some, I was beside myself with happiness. This was a manatee, a real live manatee, and it had just swum right by me to say hello! I turned to the cameras, my eyes wide, as I tried to silently express the overwhelming sense of excitement rushing through my body. I pointed to the surface, signaling the cameras to rise above the waterline so that I could direct our next move.

"Okay, we're going to head back into the spring to get up close with the manatees!" I told the cameras. The adventure was just beginning, and I signaled to Mark and Mario to follow me. We began moving further away from the boat and back in the direction of a protected cove that was heated by a natural underground spring. This ever-flowing fountain consistently pumped thousands of gallons of 72-degree water out from the earth's crust into the bay.

Kings Bay is one of the manatees' gathering grounds, and the closer to the spring we got, the more manatees surrounded us. In a sense, this spring *was* a "fountain of youth", since without it, the manatees could not survive the cold of winter. Here it was, under Ponce de Leon's feet the entire time, and he never even knew it!

My mind raced with a nervous excitement as we swam toward the spring. I led the charge as Mark and Mario followed close behind, their cameras rolling as our fins propelled us forward in the direction of a water field filled with dark floating shapes. I could feel a sense of hesitation. Here we were, bipedal strangers in a foreign watery land, and we were inviting ourselves into their world for what we hoped would be the animal encounter of a lifetime.

Would the manatees welcome us with open hearts and minds, or would they turn away from these masked invaders? My heart was pure in intention, yet my mind still asked the question, "Do we belong here?" Clearly, as humans who live on the surface, we were out of place, but I had read in books that manatees are curious creatures and absolutely love connecting with other animals, especially when those animals come in peace. When it comes to having a truly special encounter with a manatee, it's all about the manatee choosing you, and the moment it happens, your life will be changed forever.

As the dark shadows before me began to take shape, I slowed the pace of my legs, and their kicking became a gentle dance. The water around me held my body in suspension, not only physically, but also in my sense of time. In this watery domain, I felt as if time moved slower, the way it often does in a dream… and as in a dream, I could feel my body floating in slow motion toward the animals before me. I lost track of the cameras and just became one with what was happening. This was the crucial moment in which I mentally and physically prepared myself to make a connection with nature.

In front of me I could see more manatees than could be counted on a pair of hands; then from the corner of my eye, as if it had manifested from particles of silt and light, a giant drifted right past me. Its coarse skin brushed against my arm and I let my fingers dangle, the tips dragging across the gnarled and barnacle-laden creature. I felt no sense of hostility from the animal, no hesitation, no fear. Any reservations that I may have had were now completely gone as I connected with the world around me.

It was a moment of total realization and acceptance. There I was, beneath the water's surface, completely surrounded by manatees. They gently maneuvered around me, an innocent curiosity drawing us both closer to one another. I knew the cameras were there and that Mark and Mario were capturing the moments as they unfolded. However, when you can't speak during your performance, you have to learn to simply let go and be an emotionally connected natural character within the world being captured by the camera lens.

My movements came with ease as I spun in circles and danced in this watery dream amongst these ancient looking creatures. I was the new kid on the block, and it seemed as if everyone wanted to say a kind hello. Manatee after manatee drifted by, each one investigating, analyzing, and hopefully accepting me into their community.

I so desperately wanted to make a friend, if only just one single manatee who wanted to swim alongside me and guide me through this underwater world. I swam deeper into the cove, the warmth of the water pulling me in, and I pictured what it would be like to live life as a manatee...

Following along on the ocean currents in search of endless rolling plains of seagrass, warm summer afternoons spent drifting until the sun sank heavy on the western horizon... how it must feel to breach the surface and look on as the light faded out of sight. An existence so carefree, filled with peace and happiness it almost seemed impossible, yet for a manatee, that was life, and today I was living it with them.

9:38 a.m., I could feel it – my moment with a manatee was close.

Just ahead of me, a strong beam of golden sunlight cut like a saber through the gentle waves and illuminated the world in which I had lost myself. I swam toward it, drawn to its glow like a moth to the flame of a candle, and I was not the only one. This was the moment I had been dreaming of, and it was finally about to happen.

My body drifted closer, my hands outstretched as they touched the light. The creature began to appear, its wrinkled snout suddenly appearing out of the darkness as the faint light grew into a glow. In that perfect instant, we shared the same wave of light. I held my breath with my snorkel clenched snugly in my mouth; my eyes squinted through the water shield of my dive mask and locked into the doll-like eyes of the giant before me. Kindly and gently those eyes looked me over, blinked shut, and then reopened, almost as if to say hello.

I couldn't believe what was happening – then, before my mind could process what move to make next, the manatee swam right up to my face with its big squishy lips and pressed onto my mask. It was a full-blown manatee kiss!

Everything we as a team could have hoped for and everything I had spent weeks dreaming about came true in that moment.

The manatees had accepted us, and before we knew it, the fun began, as play time was suddenly in full effect.

Manatees surrounded us. It was almost impossible to choose only one to interact with on camera, as each one wanted time in the spotlight. From barrel rolls to belly rubs, we were having a blast, and the manatees put on a performance that could not have been any more elegant if it had been choreographed.

Their natural and playful curiosity drew them in toward the cameras, making Mark and Mario's job easy with plenty of subjects to film. Yet, getting shots was simultaneously incredibly difficult, since operating a camera underwater is a challenge unto itself. Just imagine trying to pull focus with a 1000-pound animal pressing its big squishy nose into your camera lens! We had no idea what kind of shots we were getting, but everyone was having so much fun that we had to just go with the flow and hope for the best.

Manatees are incredibly social animals who rely heavily on touch and sound for communication, especially between a cow and her calf. We were with numerous youngsters and were able to witness several unique behaviors including nuzzling, nursing, and cleaning. I even made friends with one unbelievably friendly and playful baby manatee who we named Douglas. 'Little Dougie' was absolutely smitten with our cameras, and it was nearly impossible to keep him from trying to kiss the lens, so I returned to the surface to update the audience on why they kept seeing the camera lens end up in the mouth of a manatee.

I spit my snorkel from my mouth as I addressed the camera, "Right now we have the most playful little baby manatee hanging around with us! He absolutely loves the cameras and is following Mark so closely that we aren't able to get any shots; he's like a giant puppy dog!"

There was no question about it, Dougie was quickly becoming the highlight of the adventure. As we swam in circles with him, it made me realize just how connected we all really are with the planet. Even at such a young age, likely less than one year, this baby was unbelievably intelligent. His emotions were magnetic, and the energy he bestowed upon the moments we spent together seemed, beyond anything else, genuine.

If I could have stayed in this watery world forever, I just might have. However, as the hours somehow slipped by, the 72-degree water was beginning to feel pretty cold, and it was time to return to the boat.

Mark, Mario, and I slowly finned our way out of the cove, past the dancing manatees and through the stark beams of light lending a magical look to the scene. It felt like the end to a perfect summer day, when Mom is calling you home for dinner but all your friends are still outside playing. I didn't

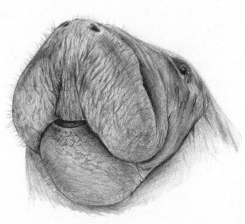

want to leave, I didn't want to say goodbye, but this was a world in which I could not survive, and my return to the surface was inevitable.

12:24 p.m.: The time for me to return to being human had arrived.

My head broke through the water's surface as my hands clasped the cold aluminum rails of the ladder leading me up from the manatee playground and back to civilization. I was sad to leave, but mustered an explosion of excitement for the cameras as I described my unbelievable encounter, delivering my closing thoughts on what I knew would make for an epic episode.

"Whoooo... HOLY SEA COW, that was awesome! It really is just like they say, swimming with manatees is truly an amazing experience! I'm Coyote Peterson; Be Brave, Stay Wild...we'll see you on the next Adventure! WOW, that was awesome!"

I walked off camera and into the cabin as Mark yelled, "CUT, THAT'S A WRAP!"

I turned back to the team and delivered a round of wet high fives, then thanked our Captain for bringing us to this majestic place.

I walked out onto the bow; the sun was now high overhead, and most of the manatees were no longer visible beneath the surface, yet I knew they were there. A light breeze blew across my face, and despite the sun's warming rays, my body began to shiver as the cold caught up with me, overcoming my excitement. It was time for some hot chocolate and a celebratory ride back to civilization. We didn't know exactly what we had captured on camera, yet we already knew that this animal encounter was unlike anything we had ever experienced before.

The sound of the boat engine firing up broke the silence that gives Kings Bay its mysterious atmosphere, and I felt reality creeping back in. With glassy eyes, I watched the sunlight ripple off the waves as we left our newfound friends behind and made our way back to a life of being human.

My heart was heavy in my chest. I was filled with gratitude for the moments I had been given, but also with a sense of loss for the manatee faces I would likely never see again, with their wrinkled noses, bristly whiskers, and black beady eyes. I knew that time would pass and certain aspects of the memory would fade, yet I hoped that perhaps they would age like a photograph in a frame, preserved beneath the glass where their yellowing edges and faded colors would become trapped in time to be forever remembered.

I knew very little about manatees before researching them to make our *Breaking Trail* episode, and I encourage you to spend a little more time learning about these incredible animals yourself. These beautiful and peaceful creatures were once nearly hunted to extinction for their value as a food source, yet have made an astounding comeback. Strong conservation efforts are constantly striving to protect these magnificent mammals and ensure hope for a bright future.

The soul of a manatee is as gentle and kind as it gets. Their ability to recognize and accept a stranger into their world is what truly sets them apart from the rest of the animal kingdom. You can see it in their eyes and you can feel it in their touch. I have had the incredible chance to work with many amazing animals, but none have I ever truly connected with as I did with the manatee that day. To have been a part of their world was like being awake in a dream; and if you ever have the chance to swim with a manatee, I promise it will change your life forever.

One day I hope that I will return to King's Bay, where my imagination will once again escape into the water and I will follow the fractals of light into the cove and once again see my friends. It's a dream I often have, and sometimes I wake up feeling as if I am still floating weightlessly in that surreal moment. Sitting up I rub my eyes, take a breath, and look back on that first visit with complete happiness in my heart. I smile, because I still have not forgotten the time that I was welcomed beneath the water's surface... to swim in the presence of giants.

Chapter 9

The Great
Salmon Adventure!

T he definition of adventure is: an exciting or unusual experience that usually involves a risky undertaking with an uncertain outcome. For as long as I can remember, I've been fascinated by the idea of adventure and have been constantly driven to push the boundaries of its very meaning.

For thousands of years, the thirst for adventure has driven men and women to push their own personal limits to extremes in a an endless quest to find, define, or become something bigger than themselves.

If you are reading this book, then you too are likely fascinated by adventure. Regardless of your age, there is a good chance that you have already had several adventures of your own. So you can understand me when I say that once you have caught the adventure bug, there is little possibility you will ever be able to escape it.

Dense clouds hung in the air, casting a gray gloom across Chilkoot Lake as a cold, never-ending drizzle of rain lightly coated my outstretched hand. As I curled my fingers into my palm, rubbing the cool water over my skin, a shiver ran down my spine. It was summer in Alaska, yet the temperatures were low enough to chill a man to the bone. I could already tell that this adventure was going to push me to my physical and mental limits, and we hadn't even gotten the cameras out of the truck yet.

Mark approached me and stepped to the edge of the water, his hiking boots sinking into the soft mud. With a sigh of concern, he looked out at the gloom and questioned the feasibility of the challenging path laid out before us.

"What do you think? Are we going after this episode, or should we push it off until the weather breaks?"

I thought about our warm cozy cabins up on the mountainside; chicken noodle soup, a good book, and my feet nestled warmly in a pair of wool socks and placed comfortably near the roaring fire place. Then I remembered that the dreary skies, light rain, and cool temperatures were ideal for locating our target animal, the sockeye salmon. Despite being unfavorable conditions for a human, the rain disturbance on the water's surface and cloudy skies make the salmon less visible to potential predators, which meant they would likely be on the move and in shallower waters.

I let out a reluctant sigh, knowing that adventures were not to be had beside warm fires in cabins. They are found through pushing the limits, defying the odds, and pressing forward in the face of risk. Believing that greatness and reward were certain to come, I made the call that any true adventurer would make.

"I think we go for this and we give it everything we've got! These conditions are perfect for finding these fish, and if we can find a school in clear shallow water, I'm confident that I'll be able to make a catch."

Despite the fact that Mark was our director and lead producer, he always respected my call when it came to finding the animals, so he prepared to rally the team.

Mario and Austin were leaning up against the truck with stocking caps on their heads, waiting in anticipation of my final call. Thermoses filled with hot chocolate kept their fingers warm as a steady loft of steam drifted into the crisp Alaskan air. It was clear they had had the same initial thoughts as I, yet like me, these guys were always ready for adventure. Mark clapped his hands, and with a smile on his face he got the excitement going.

"OK guys, Coyote says this is it. Let's get the main camera gear packed into dry bags and mount the GoPros on the kayaks. It's time to head out on the water and find those fish!"

This was shaping up to be one of our most daring expeditions to date, and the weather was only one of the many obstacles ahead of us.

Mark, Mario, Austin, and I were about to set out in two-man sea
kayaks onto Chilkoot Lake, which sits at the foot of the Takshanuk
Mountains. Spanning over three and a half miles in length and one
mile in width, its turquoise water is constantly fed by the Freebee
glacier and stays at temperatures just barely above freezing, even
during summer. Operating under special permission from the
Alaska Department of Fish and Game, our mission was to explore
the lake for small inlets housing schools of the state's most

famous fish, the sockeye salmon. If we came upon any, I was permitted to net and present a salmon for the cameras so that we could educate our audience about these incredible animals.

I secured my life vest and stepped into the front cockpit of our kayak. Clutching the double-sided paddle in my left hand, I looked over my shoulder and out at the water. Mario and Austin had already deployed from shore and were filming us at a slight distance from their kayak.

It was time for Mark and I to set off on this grand adventure!

With a heave, Mark pushed our vessel backward into the water off the gravel shore. He hurried around and down the dock, where he then quickly climbed into his cockpit. From the front of the kayak I would oversee scouting and spotting fish while he paddled, steered, and filmed from the rear. Filming this episode was going to be an incredible challenge, but we were ready to give it everything we had.

Our paddles cut through the frigid water in unison as the kayaks began to pick up speed and we headed out into the morning mist. To either side of the lake, the mountains towered above us, massive slabs of exposed stone surrounded in part by enormous trees, creating an extremely dense line of forest.

From a distance, we could see a massive glacial melt river coming off the rocks. Where this water flow eventually joined with the lake, there could potentially be a clear inlet where fish might be found. I turned around as best I could in my seat and called back to Mark, who was filming with a small waterproof action camera.

"See that water coming off the side of the mountain, that's glacial melt, and where it meets the lake the water will be incredibly clear, the perfect place to look for some salmon. Let's head over there and try to find ourselves some fish!"

It was going to take at least 20 minutes to row to where the river met the lake, and with the rain steadily coming down, the cold chill of Alaska was beginning to take its toll. The best way to get our body temperatures up was to get our blood flowing, and rowing vigorously would be the quickest way to accomplish this. As we made our way across the lake, I began to think about the fish we were searching for; I imagined hundreds of beautiful red and green streaks moving in unison just beneath the surface.

The life journey of a sockeye salmon is truly something to admire.

Once born of this very lake, their path led them away from this vast refuge, down the raging rivers, and out into the ocean. There in the great oceanic unknown they fully matured and lived their lives for several years, until eventually their biological clocks began to wind down and their natural instincts drew them back inland. Then in a mass migration, they swam with all their might up the river and returned to this very place, Chilkoot Lake. Here they would search out pockets of crystal clear water where they would reproduce, die, and return to that from which they came – a perfect circle of life.

As we rounded a bend in the lake, a massive flow of water pouring off the mountainside appeared – the river. Its power was intimidating to say the least, and it was clear that this was not a good location to find fish. The flow was so forceful that we had trouble staying in one spot as our kayaks were being pushed further out onto the lake. Mario, running camera from the cockpit of his kayak, called out, asking me for a status update.

"Hey Coyote... what are we looking at here?" he hollered over the sound of the rushing water.

At full volume, I bantered back toward the camera, "All right, this is the kind of spot that we're looking for, we've got water flowing off the side of the mountain and into the lake. Unfortunately, it's a bit too rough, and the water is very murky and deep. If I can't see the fish, I can't catch them. Let's keep moving along the side of the mountain and see if we can find something better!"

I dug my oar into the water, propelling the kayak forward, and we continued our quest for clear water along the outer reaches of the lake.

We paddled north along the eastern side of the lake and explored cove after cove, yet there were no signs of fish. The harsh nature of the elements made the adventure exciting; however, after several hours in the cold rain, all I could think about was how nice a bowl of hot chicken noodle soup was going to be when the day was over.

I knew the fish were out here, literally hundreds, if not thousands of them were just beneath the murky surface, yet it seemed they were nowhere to be found.

I often rely on my senses to help me find animals, and my sense of sight is always the first tool I use. So you can imagine how discouraging it was to spend hours in the cold and not see a single fish. Then, just when it seemed all hope was lost, another one of my senses kicked in.

My ears picked up a sound from across the lake – I heard the iconic cry of a bald eagle. It's a shrill high-pitched cackle, not what you would expect from such a large bird, but in that moment, something clicked in my mind. Eagles eat salmon! Could it be possible that this giant bird of prey was in the process of hunting for the exact same animal we were hoping to net and get up close to the cameras?

Keeping a steady balance, I carefully turned myself around so that I could reach my adventure pack. Unzipping the top pocket, I quickly removed a pair of binoculars, checked the lenses for water spots, and then raised them to my eyes. I adjusted the focus and my line of sight until I could see clearly and then began scanning the tree line on the far side of the lake.

The eagle called again. Perfect timing, as the sound allowed me to realign the binocular lenses in the exact direction needed; within seconds I spotted the bird. It was a juvenile and had not yet developed the magnificent white head and tail.

It's completely dark coloration made it look like a giant hawk, but sure enough, I was looking directly at a bald eagle. The massive raptor called again, spread its wings, and dropped from its perch. Swooping down toward the water, it momentarily hovered near the surface before finding a perch on a lower branch of the tree. I followed the bird with my binoculars, and it led my gaze straight toward a cove that cut back into the dense forest.

I studied the shoreline with precision and spotted several other eagles hidden amongst the dense trees. Counting four in total, I knew that these predatory birds had only one thing on their minds... FISH. This could be the perfect spot to find, and if we were lucky, catch a sockeye salmon.

Aiming directly toward the eagles, we quickly began paddling across the lake for the shore. Excitement was in the air, and as we drew closer to making landfall I saw the first signs of salmon.

With a smile on my face, I addressed Mario's camera and delivered an update for the audience, "There are four eagles up in this tree that have led us straight to the fish. Back in this cove I can see a bunch of dorsal fins splashing; there are about a hundred salmon tucked back in this cove. Guys, we have found salmon! We have been rowing this entire lake, and lo and behold, it was finding eagles that brought us to the fish. This of course makes sense, because the eagles are here feeding... but guys, we need to be careful, because this is also a prime spot for grizzlies to come down and feast. We're going set up a base camp and then strategize how we are going to catch one of these fish."

I turned to Mark and gave him a high five with my paddle; the excitement was electric. We had finally found fish, which meant that we were going to get a shot at catching one; a feat far easier said than done!

We quietly paddled away from the cove so that we would not disturb the salmon with our presence. Cautiously, we drifted our kayaks up to an embankment just a few hundred yards away and scouted for bears from the water's edge. At first glance, I was unable to see any of the predatory mammals, so I carefully stepped out of the kayak and onto the shore.

My water boots squished into the soggy ground, a saturated mix of mud and moss. After being locked in the portal of a kayak for several hours, my legs felt numb, so I leaned on my oar for balance. Slowly I scanned from left to right, peering through the dense maze of tree trunks and large leafy ferns. I could feel my heart rate increasing as the full weight of the situation sank in; this was bear territory. The first thing wilderness survival training teaches is to make loud noises in a situation like this, so I called out into the forest to alert and hopefully scare off any bears if they were present.

"HEY BEAR, HEY BEAR!" I hollered at the top of my lungs into the Alaskan wilderness, while also clapping my hands as loudly as I possibly could. The sound echoed through the trees, and while part of me expected to hear the crashing of a large animal running off through the underbrush, the forest remained silent. To my delight, it seemed as if no bears were present, yet with continued suspicion, I slowly crept up the shoreline. No more than a few yards from our kayaks, I stumbled upon the haunting remains of a previously consumed salmon.

Piles of rib bones, scales, and toothed jaws were definitive evidence that this had once been the dinner table of a brown bear. Nothing to be worried about, though; this kill was weeks if not months old, so I signaled for the crew to come ashore. Mario was rolling camera from his kayak, so I addressed the safety of our current situation for the benefit of the worried minds of anyone watching.

"This spot's pretty perfect, but be aware that we are definitely in bear territory right now. I gave it a quick scout, made some noise, and shouted and clapped my hands – just trying to alert any animals that we are now here. Remember, if there are salmon, there are definitely bears, so just be aware."

I reached out and grabbed the front of Mario and Austin's kayak, and with a heave I pulled them onto the embankment. I could still feel my heart racing. Nothing is more nerve-wracking than setting your camp in an area that is clearly visited by bears.

Our first order of business was to scout the salmon cove from a controlled position on land so that we could formulate a plan of approach using our kayaks from the water. In a single file line, Mark, Mario, Austin, and I began to move in the direction of the cove to get a closer look.

The foliage was dense, and fallen trees made our route incredibly difficult as we were forced to zigzag around stumps and clamber over and under the remains of toppled giants. We were clearly not the first creatures to navigate this maze, as clumps of bear fur were frequently to be found snagged on some of the jagged branches.

With the cameras rolling, I pulled a honey-colored tuft from an overhanging branch and held it out toward the lens of the camera. No words were needed, as just the sight of this fur spoke volumes about the danger that we were in. Continuing forward, our eyes soon witnessed paw prints in the mud and even bear scat (more commonly known as bear poop) littered along the game trail.

Now you may be asking yourself, 'Coyote, why weren't you and the crew making loud noises at this point? Shouldn't you be alerting any possible bears in the area, just like when you landed your kayaks?' In theory, yes; however, shouts and clapping this close to the cove could startle and scare the fish. So, while it was incredibly risky, staying stealthy in this dangerous situation was necessary; but it left us feeling very nervous as we climbed through the underbrush.

Finally, the timber maze came to an end, and we emerged onto the crested knoll of the salmon cove. Looking down into the crystal clear water, we could immediately see dozens of these magnificent fish slowly navigating the current of the stream. They were beautiful. Brilliant crimson bodies, sharp and streamlined, occasionally darted from spot to spot with incredible agility and elegance.

The females, which are slightly smaller in size, patiently guarded their nests while the larger males faced off in battles of territorial dominance. This natural behavior was incredible to witness, and Mario took the opportunity to capture this rarely seen moment in the lives of these animals on camera.

We were incredibly excited, and the setup was perfect. This particular cove was structured in almost the exact way I had envisioned: a calm flow of glacial melt water pouring from the

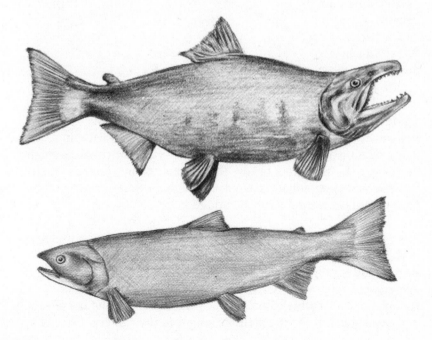

mountain that funneled into a protected pool, which was slightly partitioned off from the lake. It was ideal for the fish and picture-perfect for our cameras.

While studying the lay of the land we formulated our plan. In theory, execution of the catch was rather simple. We would slowly row both kayaks toward the cove; Mark and I first as Mario and Austin followed. I would ride perched in the front cockpit of our kayak, large fishing net in hand, and gently step into the clear water just as we entered the cove. With precision, I would slink toward the salmon that were cornered in the shallower water near the back of the cove. Once I was close enough, I would plunge the net into the water and scoop up a fish!

With our plan in place, we snuck back through the timber maze and toward base camp to ready the kayaks.

This was going to be an incredibly difficult animal capture to get on camera, as Mark was forced to leave our main camera at base camp. The reason for this was that when I got out of the kayak to enter the water, there was a realistic chance I could flip Mark into the icy bath. Let me tell you what you don't want to do... dunk an expensive camera in a lake! So, we planned to shoot the approach and salmon catch using small waterproof action cameras. In the event that I actually caught a fish, Mark was to row back to base camp, grab the main camera, and then quickly navigate the timber maze back to the cove where we waited with the netted fish.

Mental preparation is an important part of what I do, so with closed eyes I clenched the handle of the net in my hands and visualized myself netting one of these monster sockeyes. Mark fired up his camera and caught me in a candid moment as he asked what I thought my odds were of actually landing one. I opened my eyes and quickly described the plan, looking into the camera. I ended by saying, "I think I have about a 75% chance of landing one of these fish on the first attempt!"

I had claimed some rather favorable odds, but given the shallow nature of the cove, the clarity of the water, and the large number of fish present... my confidence and ambition were ready to challenge my talent for catching animals. I should mention that almost everyone we spoke with from Alaska thought that what I was about to attempt was near impossible... but as you may have gathered by now, "impossible" is not a word in this team's vocabulary.

We climbed into the kayaks, cameras rolling; this was it – time to catch a salmon!

From the lake, we could see back into the cove, where dorsal fins breached the surface as they darted back and forth. These aquatic animals are incredibly in tune with their environment, and at even the slightest disturbance, they would quickly flee back into the lake away from any potential danger. Stealth was absolutely necessary.

Mark smoothly rowed behind me, aiming the kayak right into the cove. Mario and Austin rowed in from the shore side of the lake; we hoped that between the two boats we would actually flush more fish back into the cove, as opposed to scaring them out into deeper water. However, this did not prove to be the case, as once we neared the cove's opening, the fish began to scatter in a flurry around the sides of our kayaks.

As we entered the mouth of the cove, salmon started to flash by like bolts of red and green lightning, darting past us one after another. With a raised fist, I signaled Mark to cease our forward momentum, and the kayak drifted to a halt. I scanned the water and analyzed the current plan of attack. No more than 50 feet ahead, I could see the water was alive with salmon that had not yet noticed our presence.

I took a deep breath and slowly lifted my right foot over the side of the kayak, slipping it into the water. The incredible shock of the nearly freezing temperature hit me like a bolt of electricity, sending chills through my entire body. "YIKES, that is freezing cold!" I thought to myself as I balanced my body and pulled my left foot out of the kayak, submerging it beneath the surface. I was now in the frigid world of the sockeye, with my net grasped tightly in my hands and focus in my eyes.

Wiggling my toes in my boots, I tried to adjust to the cold as my feet navigated the slippery river rocks. It was a strange feeling, the combination of cold, adrenaline, and the immense pressure to net one of these fish. As I ventured further into the cove, my presence became apparent to the salmon. They began darting from side to side as I neared their stronghold. A pair to my right darted for an escape, and I lunged toward them with outstretched arms. Thrusting the net into the water, I could feel the front rim hit rock and bounce back toward me. The fish zipped past me before the net even hit the surface of the water. MISS!

My sharp movement had disturbed a few other fish, and they scattered toward my left side, as there was now a clear escape route. Already off balance, I threw my body in their direction, and with all my might I swooped the net down into the water after them. A wave of icy water flooded up over my arms as the fish avoided the net with incredible agility. MISS NUMBER TWO!

Then on the right side, a lone male darted past so fast I couldn't even balance myself enough to make an attempt. The freezing cold water bit at the tips of my fingers as I struggled to keep my grip on the aluminum handle of the net. My arms were soaked, and with the water nearly waist deep, I could feel my body slowing in reaction to the paralyzing cold. I shook my head, regaining my composure and focus.

Several fish still nervously darted back and forth in the cove ahead of me, but I knew the 'lunge and swipe method' was just simply too slow and cumbersome. I could feel the looming cloud of defeat growing over me when suddenly a small movement caught my eye. Tucked back in the far corner, I could see the dark shadow of a lone fish hiding under the embankment.

Could this be my chance at redemption? My probability of success was dropping with each passing moment. With bated breath, my team watched through the eye of the camera as the action played out.

Now I had a target, a fish who felt hidden and who would hopefully stay locked in hiding as opposed to darting for the refuge of the open lake. The remaining fish blurred in my peripheral vision. As I took a few steps forward, they darted to the far left and right, playing the sides of the cove to their advantage as they made their break for escape. My target was still holding strong. I was close now, less than ten feet away. I clenched my hands around the handle of the net; this was it, my last chance to net a sockeye salmon!

The moment played out in my mind as if it happened in slow motion.

I lunged forward, propelling my hands with precision and accuracy as the rim of the net broke through the surface and plunged into the icy water. In a startle, the fish exploded with power, and suddenly a wave of water splashed out from under the embankment, forcing my eyes closed. I heaved upward with all my might, and in that instant, I felt the weight of something within the confines of the net. With a victorious holler, I pulled the net up and out of the water... and there above the surface, we beheld a giant sockeye salmon!

"I DID IT, I CAUGHT ONE!" I yelled back to the cameras; "Got one, got one... WHOO! There we go, got one! All right, it's strong, it's heavy. Get the boats back..."

The fish was fighting with all its might to escape the net; feeling its strength and power was incredible! My body was rushing with a pure mix of adrenaline and excitement. If the fish didn't somehow escape, we were going to get an episode out of this epic adventure.

According to plan, Mark quickly rowed his kayak out of the cove and paddled along the shoreline back to base camp. He retrieved his camera and raced toward the cove through the timber maze. During this time, Austin and Mario stayed close to me with the camera rolling as I addressed the current state of affairs.

"Holy cow, can't believe I got one... that is a good fish right there. I want to keep the fish as calm as I can – you see it there just swimming down in the water?"

Mario directed his camera down toward the surface, and sure enough, there in the confines of the net, I safely held the big fish underwater.

"I played it absolutely perfectly, they were darting left and right, there was no way I was going to be able to get one in the deep water so I played up underneath the embankment, and that's how I was able to nab it. A full-grown male... I don't think we could have landed a more perfect fish! YES!"

I gave Mario a big high five just as Mark returned with the additional camera gear. He directed us to move back into the cove so we could begin filming the presentation portion of the episode. I slowly moved the salmon through the water. It was necessary to handle the fish with great care; these animals are incredibly fragile, and my goal was to put as little stress on it as possible.

I needed to keep the fish submerged for a good portion of the video, which would require me to remain in the nearly freezing water. By then, I had been in almost 10 minutes, and I was losing feeling in my toes, feet, legs, and even my hands and fingers. I was beginning to worry about the onset of hypothermia, a medical emergency that occurs when one's body loses heat faster than it can be produced, causing a dangerously low body temperature. It can set in rather quickly, so we needed to get the shots and get me out of the water as fast as possible.

Near the back of the cove, I saw the remains of a tree trunk and root structure that we decided would be the perfect place to set the scene and get to work. Slowly I lifted the salmon out of the net and revealed the animal in its full glory to the camera for the first time; then I began presenting, "Look at that salmon, how unbelievably gorgeous is this animal? Now, the way that you can immediately identify this as a dominant male is you'll notice the quintessential green head, the hooked jaw with those massive teeth, and this large ridge on top of the back which develops as these fish mature. You may be wondering to yourself, is this fish really scaly? No, it's not, this fish is incredibly smooth and very difficult to hold onto, which is why I'm keeping it partially in the net. These fish are so fast and so strong. The way that they migrate from the ocean and move up the rivers to the spawning grounds is just so impressive. In my opinion this is the most beautiful salmon species in the world!"

Our time with the animal was incredibly limited, and what set this apart from most other animal encounters was that there was some important data we needed to collect. Part of the requirements of the permit granted to us by the Alaska Department of Fish and Game was that we were to collect biometrics of the fish. This meant I needed to take recordings of the animal's length and weight.

Gently setting the fish back into the net, I reached for my pack and began unzipping the main compartment. My fingers were now completely numb and turning pink, and I could barely open the pack; it was apparent that the cold was taking hold of me. Early signs of hypothermia were beginning to set in, which was a stern warning that we needed to move quickly before my situation deteriorated any further.

Mario helped me open my pack to remove a measuring tape and scale to record the fish's length and weight. I crouched down into the ice-cold water and placed the tip of the measuring tape along the animal's jawline to get the length first. I looked up at the camera and described exactly what I was doing.

"Now, I want to be as accurate as I possibly can be here, tip of the snout down to where the tail fin connects to the body... wow, 24 inches, that is a two-foot salmon right there!"

Next, I gently inserted the scale into a crease between the salmon's jaw and gills, a standard method for weighing a fish, and lifted it into the air, calling out the weight.

"He is at nine pounds, that is a pretty good-sized salmon!" I set the fish back down into the submerged net; our data had been recorded, and it was almost time for its release.

I noticed a lighter coloration toward the back of the fish's tail; I felt it was an interesting visual difference and important fact to note, so I addressed the camera, "Now, these fish are at the end of their life cycle, let me show you something very interesting here..."

I lifted the fish back up out of the net, exposing its body to the camera, cold water running down its slippery sides and through my fingers. It fought my grip with incredible strength, yet I was able to calm the animal and showcase its morphing tail.

"Look at the tail, see how it's much lighter in coloration? These fish actually begin to deteriorate as they move up stream. You can see there are some gnarled areas on the back of the tail, but what's most distinct is the light coloration in the tail as compared to the rest of the body; this is a sign that the fish is at the end of its life cycle. It's kind of gross and also sad, but these fish actually disintegrate as they age and eventually die. When this fish does finally pass away, it will become food for a bear or an eagle, returning to this amazing Alaskan wilderness in the form of nutrition for the other animals that are out here."

From a conservation standpoint, this was an important note to make, since we wanted the audience to understand that even though it was sad to think about an animal passing away, in death they provided life for the other wildlife that called this environment home. We took one last look at the salmon, rolled camera on some underwater footage and concluded that the time to release the fish back into the wild had arrived. I delivered my outro:

"How awesome was this, braving the wilds of Alaska and actually netting a sockeye salmon… I'm Coyote Peterson, Be Brave, Stay Wild…We'll see you on the next adventure"!

I gently placed the fish down into the water, submerging it below the surface. I could feel the animal breathing as it brought water in through its mouth and flushed it over its gills. I loosened my grip on the sides of the fish's body and released it into the cove. He was now free.

My body was freezing cold, and as I stood up, water dripping from my arms and hands, I clenched my fingers into fists, trying to regain some feeling. With my eyes fixated on the fish, I stood watching as this beautiful creature swam forward and gradually disappeared into the deeper water. As he rejoined his kind, I felt an overwhelming sense of happiness knowing that our fish was returning to the wild unharmed.

As a team, we all cheered in celebration and shared in a round of high fives and congratulations, knowing that an amazing episode of *Breaking Trail* had just wrapped.

You never know how the footage will cut together in postproduction, yet we knew that something amazing had happened that day in the Alaskan wilderness. When we imagined catching a sockeye salmon with a net, we knew it would certainly be difficult and maybe even impossible. Yet, I managed to pull it off, making this one of the greatest animal encounters of my life.

With my body shivering uncontrollably, Mario helped me hike through the timber maze as we navigated back to base camp. A combination of dry clothes and jumping jacks halted the threatening onset of hypothermia. My fingers and toes, which had turned completely white, were now regaining color, feeling, and dexterity. I had pushed my body to its limits and risked it all to see this adventure through from start to finish, but it was totally worth it.

With warm blood now flowing through my body, we broke down our base camp, packed up the kayaks, and shoved off back onto the lake toward home. In silence, we rowed across the water. I think we were all lost in our thoughts and feeling a great appreciation for the grand adventure we were concluding.

My mind drifted to the last moments I had spent with the sockeye salmon as he swam from my fingertips and returned to the lake. A wave of happiness blanketed me with the knowledge that our mission was an incredible success. I found my heart overflowing with gratitude as nature had allowed me to spend time in the presence of such a brave and well-traveled creature. I hung on the final image of that big fish slowly disappearing into the shadows, knowing that this adventure was a moment in my life that I would never forget.

Chapter 10

The
ShadowStalker!

O ver the course of this book, we have embarked upon many of my bravest adventures and animal encounters, everything from prehistoric looking snapping turtles to magnificent sockeye salmon, enormous brown bears, and adorable Florida manatees.

Then of course we ran into, or should I say we did our best NOT to run into, some of the wild's most notorious biological landmines. There were venomous reptiles like the western diamondback rattlesnake and countless arachnids like the black widow and giant desert centipede, as well as PLENTY of scorpions.

Whether they were big or small, safe or deadly, scary or heartwarming, all of these animals have made possible the most exciting moments of my life, which through this book have become memories that we now share together.

However, I am often asked, "What is the *most* memorable animal encounter you have ever had?" Honestly, it's a very tough question to answer... but there is always one dark night in the rainforests of Costa Rica that stands out in my mind, an encounter that to this day I still remember in complete disbelief.

The night that I came face to face... with the shadow stalker!

Sitting on the back porch of my jungle hut, I watched as the giant golden sun disappeared behind the mountains; with its exit, the landscape welcomed in the darkness of night. I pulled on my boots and yanked tight the laces, slung a backpack over my shoulder, and reached for my weathered cowboy hat. My watch read 8:35 p.m. That meant it was time to connect with the crew and head out into the rainforest for another adventure. Earlier in the day a thunderous rainstorm had pushed through the region, which told us that it should be a great evening to search for creatures. Already the darkness was alive with the sounds of insects and frogs; a natural orchestra of wild music that was going to make an epic background score for our expedition. I closed my eyes and focused my hearing, soaking in all of the sounds of night.

Suddenly I heard the approach of hiking boots sloshing through the muddy underbrush. The gait was quick, the approach purposeful – then the sound abruptly stopped. I listened carefully, and then with a "WHAP!" I heard something smack the side of my jungle hut. I already knew who it was – Mario! He had likely seen a catchable critter that was hunting on the side of my hut. The only question yet to be answered was, had he caught it?

From around the corner he appeared with a closed hand outstretched into the beam of his flashlight. The smile on his face said it all, yet I had to ask.

"What did you catch?"

Slowly he opened the cage formed by his fingers, revealing a reptilian creature within his clutches.

"It's a little Mediterranean Gecko... that's two points, right?" he asked with a smirk.

Over the years, Mario and I have had an ongoing "friendly" competition whenever we are on location; '*Who Can Catch More Creatures?*' We ranked them on a point scale from one to five based on the difficulty of the catch and the species of animal caught.

For example: A lightning bug would be one point, since it was simple and safe to catch. Something like a white–lipped mud turtle, which is aquatic, quick, and can give you a pretty nasty bite, was ranked at 5 points. The Mediterranean Gecko, while quick and agile, is incredibly common and very safe to handle. So yeah, two points, Mario!

Sensing Mario's state of distraction and a clear path to freedom, the lizard sprang from the open palm of his hand and leapt onto a nearby leaf, from which it scurried into the underbrush. With the lizard gone, Mario's focus returned to his purpose for approaching my hut in the first place.

"Mark wants to get moving… we are going to head north into the rainforest along the edge of the ravine. It could be a great place to come across a fer-de-lance or an eyelash viper, especially with all the rain that moved through earlier. You ready to go?"

I placed my cowboy hat on my head and adjusted the brim. My adventure outfit was now complete, and I answered Mario's lingering question, "Yep, ready for action… let's find some snakes!"

I picked up my snake tongs, a tool I often use to handle venomous snakes, and together we headed off into the night.

Filming episodes of *Breaking Trail* under the cover of darkness is my absolute favorite way to capture animal encounters on camera. There is always a heightened sense of adventure and anticipation when we are filming at night. Sounds become amplified, and shadows challenge your vision while you search for hiding creatures; and every step you take, if you are not careful, could walk you straight into the fangs or stinger of a deadly biological landmine. Your senses are always on overdrive at night, prompting your imagination to run wild, since you never know what sort of dangers lurk in the dark. On this particular evening, I felt as if something incredible was going to happen, yet I don't think any of us could have ever dreamed what would soon unfold before us.

The surrounding trees were massive, covered in hanging vines and mosses which in turn cast eerie shadows against our flashlight beams as we cautiously moved deeper into the underbrush. The air was thick with humidity, and even under the cover of darkness, the temperature was still a balmy ninety degrees Fahrenheit. I could feel the sweat building on my brow line before it beaded and ran a course down the side of my face. Sweating at night is one of the strangest feelings, because one would normally associate such a bodily function with sunlight beating down or the exertion of heavy physical activity. However, we were simply walking in a dark rainforest, yet here we were, dripping with sweat!

I tried to keep my focus on the environment, yet it became difficult, since I was constantly having to wipe my face with a handkerchief. The humidity was so thick you could practically breathe in the droplets of water that hung in the air. My eyes squinted as I tried my best to distinguish the difference between gnarled bark on the tree trunks and something that might be a creature cleverly camouflaged on its surface. Spotting animals in the dark, even with a flashlight, can be incredibly difficult. The human eye was not designed to operate with precision or accuracy in the shadow zone and its complex variations of darkness.

The shadow zone.

It is a place you have heard me describe before, which I define as the space between the light and the dark; a gray area that has just enough illumination for the human eye to see, but also enough darkness for an animal to feel hidden.

You see, humans are diurnal creatures, which means that our eyes, despite their complex design of cones and rods, are best used by the light of day. When our eyes are put to the test against a pitch black rainforest devoid of light, we are left nearly blind.

However, the opposite is true for most animals in the rainforest.

Many of these creatures were designed to be nocturnal, which means that they have excellent vision in the dark. It is here they perform their best and survive under the hidden cover of night.

Snakes, tree frogs, spiders... and even rainforest mammals like kinkajous and coatimundi are perfect examples. Not only do they use the darkness to stay hidden from predators, but if they are predators themselves, they use the darkness as an advantage to help stalk and hunt their prey.

I have always believed that it is a true art form to train one's eyes to properly adjust to the dark... to see beyond the glow of a flashlight and into the shadow zone. Training your eyes to see into this middle area can really help you spot animals at night. If an animal finds itself hiding in this zone, it is likely to stay in place and not flee.

Why is that, you ask? It's simple. If an animal recognizes that it has been illuminated by a flashlight its next best defense is to rely on its natural camouflage to keep it hidden, and that only works if the animal stays completely still. This allows me as a naturalist to slowly approach the animal and hopefully catch it so that it can be presented for the cameras.

Often, I will practice the art of seeing into the shadow zone by simply pointing my flashlight toward the ground. Standing still in one place for several minutes, I let my eyes adjust to the mixture of light and darkness that surrounds me, and I focus on seeing beyond the glow of the light. However, I never turn the light completely off, because in the rainforests of Costa Rica, even if you are standing still, you never know what sort of danger may be lurking amidst the leaf litter at your feet or on the palm fronds just overhead. It's important to be constantly aware of your surroundings.

I heard Mario call back toward me from up ahead as I stood in the pitch black.

"Hey Coyote, come here, you gotta see this spider… it's HUGE!"

With my focus on adapting to the darkness distracted, I quickly pointed my flashlight toward the team and walked in the direction of Mario's call, my light beam quickly scanning the ground before my feet. You never know where the next biological landmine may be waiting, and with snakes always on the stalk and slither, you are wise to watch your every step.

My eyes squinted in reaction to the bright lights; Mark and Chance had already begun filming the eight-legged creature, which happily chewed on its not so lucky prey. The spider's attention was on its dinner and not us, which was good news, because this was the infamous wandering spider.

My flashlight beam cast a warm glow over the arachnid as I slowly leaned in for a dangerously close look.

"WOW... look at the way its mandibles and fangs work independently to tear apart the victim. I can't exactly tell what it's eating, but it looks like some kind of leaf katydid or small grasshopper. Ugh, you can see how the venom has completely broken down the insect's exoskeleton and turned it into a ball of mushy goo! Gross, this spider is feasting on a bug milkshake!"

Mark directed a valid question to me as my pointer finger inched closer to the spider's face while I described the chewing action.

"So, Coyote, your finger is getting a little close there... this looks dangerous. That spider's venomous, right?"

Pulling my hand back slowly so as not to startle the spider and instigate a lunging bite, I controlled my excitement as reality checked in.

"Yeah, good point, Mark... and yes, this is quite possibly the most venomous spider we could have encountered tonight. They have an incredibly potent neurotoxic venom that not only causes extreme pain but which can result in a loss of muscle control and serious breathing problems. A bite from this spider would likely put me in the hospital, and we are a long way from civilization. This creepy-crawly is best admired from a safe distance, so we will let it go about having dinner and..."

Suddenly, from the darkness, the sound of footsteps running through the underbrush caused me to halt my presentation mid-sentence; my heart figuratively jumped out of my chest. I quickly turned in the direction of the sound and in complete disbelief witnessed an ocelot darting across the light beams and then disappearing back into the shadowy darkness.

I looked at the crew with bewilderment – I could not believe my own two eyes!

The ocelot is one of central America's most elusive wild cats.

These medium-sized felines are nocturnal predators that rely on their incredible night vision to navigate the darkness, which allows them to stalk the forest completely unnoticed. They are nearly silent as they hunt and often use their mastery of the shadows to sneak up on unsuspecting prey.

This sudden encounter was remarkable because these cats are so rarely seen by humans!

Then, without warning... *pitter patter, pitter patter, pitter patter...* the sound of paws in the underbrush was coming closer in the darkness and heading straight for us. I could feel my heart beat faster as my mind prepared for the worst.

'What if this cat has been stalking us the entire night, waiting for the perfect moment to attack?!'

I'll admit, I was a little scared. I mean, this was a wild jungle cat, and it was literally charging straight at us! These animals are typically skittish and elusive, often doing their best to avoid humans. However, this one had a playful curiosity that was very unusual.

The sound slowed from an attack approach to a walk, and then, like a phantom from the shadows, the animal's shape materialized before us. The cat lowered its head and smelled the air to investigate, took several timid steps forward, and then stopped in the furthest reaches of the light and stared right at us. Its eyes reflected the light with a haunting glow as we all held our breath, frozen in place awaiting the animals next move.

I strained to quickly adjust my eyes. Thinking that this might be but a fleeting glance, I wanted to soak in as much of the sight as I could before the cat disappeared into the night.

There it was, coated with black and white spots... an ocelot! It kept its head ducked low, obeying a natural instinct cats have when they are curious or hunting prey. Slowly it stepped forward, stalking in the shadow zone, just under thirty feet from us.

I crouched lower to its level. This could be considered extremely dangerous, but something inside of me felt as if this cat was in a curious mood and NOT looking to attack. As it cautiously walked closer, I could tell it was a juvenile, which means that it was basically a teenager and likely out for an evening stroll. Previous fears of being mauled by this jungle cat quickly diminished, and I just hoped that someone was rolling a camera so that we had proof of seeing this beautiful creature.

Then, without warning, the cat lifted its head, and with a few strides that ended in a bounding leap, it sprang straight toward me. Plop! It landed just before my feet, and with an outstretched paw began to whap playfully at my boot laces.

I was literally speechless...

Coyote Peterson at a complete loss for words. Knowing I had to do something, as the cameras were now definitely rolling, my natural instinct was to look up and deliver a profound statement. Yet all I could muster was, "WHOA... that's a wild ocelot, and it's right here at my feet, look at that, how cool is that!?"

It was immediately apparent that this ocelot was friendly and more interested in making me into its playmate than an item on its dinner menu.

Mark and Chance, who were completely bewildered themselves, briefly cut the cameras, and we quickly strategized what to do next. Playing at my feet was a once in a lifetime opportunity to get one of the rarest rainforest mammals in front of the cameras, and we had to act fast. Mark immediately took direction of the scene to ensure that we could get the cameras back up and rolling as quickly as possible.

"Mario, set up the lights there next to that fallen tree, Chance, you try and get as much B-roll as possible, stay tight on the cat and just keep rolling. Coyote... well, just do what you do and try to keep the cat's attention as long as you can! Here we go guys, let's film an ocelot!"

I sat down next to the log, and Mark called "Action!" I quickly recapped for the audience what had just happened and looked around for the ocelot. The sound of its paws pattering on the forest floor could be heard, but I needed to bring its attention back in front of the cameras. Holding on to my snake tongs, which have a few jangly metal parts, I rattled it against the tree, creating a sound that no curious cat could resist.

"The ocelot seemed to like my snake tongs. Let's see if this will get it back... wait for this." Mere seconds after I began making the noise, the cat appeared, almost as if out of thin air, right next to my leg.

"Oh, there you are!" I exclaimed with excitement to see my new jungle friend.

With an outstretched paw, the feline jabbed at the end of the snake tongs. The speed and agility of the animal was incredibly impressive. One moment she was in front of me pawing at the tongs, and the next she was behind me playfully attacking my arm.

Wrapping its front paws around my forearm, the ocelot gripped onto me and began gnawing on my leather wrist bracelet with its teeth. I could feel the scratchy texture of its tongue on my skin. If you have ever been licked by a house cat, then you know it feels like being rubbed with soft sandpaper. This felt like that only much rougher and with three times the power; it almost felt like the cat was going to lick my skin off!

"Ahhh, she's attacking my arm!" I cried out with a laugh.

This was completely crazy; a wild ocelot was chewing on my arm!

I picked the cat up and held her in the air, a method I have used in the past to get smaller mammals to calm down and turn their attention toward me. It worked for a second, but then like most cats it turned around in my hands asking to be put down, so back to the forest floor the cat went. Clearly this scene was going to play out according to the ocelot's rules and not under the direction of the humans with cameras.

"Well, I guess the cat's going to be all over the place for this scene, let's see... what else do I have for you to play with?"

Keeping the attention of the ocelot wasn't going to be easy. I knew the best bet for getting it to stay close by, and hopefully in front of the cameras, was to simply improvise with anything I had readily available to draw it in. I have always had luck getting house cats to play with me, so it only made sense that playing in the same fashion with a wild cat would yield similar results.

My adventure pack was full of clasps, buckles, and zippers, so I unclipped it from my chest, swung my arms free of the shoulder straps, and plopped it with a rattling thud onto the log. Instantly the young jungle predator sprang to attack the pack, and I began talking to it with a playful tone.

"Look at that, look at that... Want to wrestle with the pack? Get it, get it!"

My tactic was working. The ocelot was lying on its back batting at the bag with its oversized paws. I might as well have been playing with a supersized tabby cat batting at a toy mouse on a string! This was my first chance to incorporate some ocelot facts into the developing episode, so I wracked my brain and the first thing I could think of... was its beautiful spotted coat.

"Take a look at that coloration, this cat blends so perfectly into its environment – all this cryptic patterning allows it to stay hidden in the shadows as it's moving through the dense jungle foliage."

I could see that putting a pause in playing to address the cameras was not keeping the ocelot's attention, as the cat spun to its feet and prepared to spring from the log. So, I quickly grabbed ahold of the wild animal beneath its front legs and once again lifted it like a house cat.

With a swooping playful swing, I held the young animal in front of me. This was risky, because the ocelot had either accepted me or it hadn't. I prepared for a face full of claws but was thankfully met with warm, excited purring. The ocelot began pawing at my face with its big squishy feet as it gently gnawed on my fingers. The teeth were incredibly sharp and felt like needle points in my skin as they clasped down on my hands. I could certainly tell this cat's pawing and bites were playful as the cat continued to coo and purr, biting just softly enough to not break skin. At this point it was all fun and games, and I may as well have been a littermate!

I did my best to describe what was happening, "A paw to the face, a paw to the face... Watch my eyes, those claws are sharp, buddy!

The cat simply loved to bat at my face, and once again I had her attention, so stealing a moment to reel out another ocelot fact was instinctual. This time I wanted to address the cat's weight, as I now had it clasped in my hands. Holding the animal up and out in front of me, I said, "This ocelot is only about half grown right now, but it weighs around 25 pounds..."

This was all the fact giving that would be tolerated, and before I knew it, a paw whacked the side of my face. One might think this ocelot was trained to interrupt on cue the delivery of lines to a camera! Returning my attention to the cat was what it wanted, so I happily obliged. Small bites to the cheek and ear, licks of its tongue, and continued pats of approval from its paws kept the encounter spontaneous. I never knew what to expect next and warned the cat not to go for my throat with those bites. Mention of a throat bite gave me the immediate idea to talk about an ocelot's kill strategy when hunting.

"These cats are lethal when fully grown and are capable of taking down almost anything that is out here in the Costa Rican rainforest. All they have to do is run, leap, and sink in those front claws, hold on tight, and then with a bite to the neck – BOOM, they have a meal!"

This was a very valid point. Using agility and speed, a full-grown ocelot can even kill a deer that is several times its own weight. However, they primarily hunt for and feast on smaller forest vertebrates like mice, lizards, birds, and if they can catch them, tree dwelling animals like sloths and kinkajous.

Keeping the flow of the scene going, Mark asked me, "So, Coyote, is this rare?" I responded, "This is probably the most unique encounter I have ever had with an animal."

At that moment, the ocelot began grappling onto my back and clawing at my leather hat; it was attempting to climb up onto my head so it could literally sit on me! My instinct was to cinch my eyes shut so that they wouldn't accidentally get snagged by its claws. Like a house cat, the ocelot's front claws can retract, which means that most of the time they are protected within a skin sheath. They are only deployed when needed, whether to catch and hold onto prey, or to climb something like a tree, or in this case a Coyote.

Up to this point, all the pawing had been playful and free of claws. Now that the cat had a mission, it needed to use its claws to hold onto my back and shoulders as it climbed. Boy, was I able to feel how razor-sharp those claws were, and I froze with pain as I could feel them digging into my shoulders.

The scene was getting out of control as clearly the ocelot was playing for the lead role.

"Now just so everyone knows, this is not a captive animal, right?" Mark asked.

"No, this is a wild ocelot, 100% wild. Now, I would never recommend that you go out into the rainforest and try to get this close to an ocelot, because if it didn't want to play, it could really do some serious damage."

I was having trouble presenting any sort of fluid thoughts or really keeping my mind centered on ocelot facts with claws digging into my skin. The cat simply wanted to have fun, and I knew that the most important thing was to just let the scene unfold naturally, as long as the cat didn't get too rough and I could endure the pain.

Even the crew found themselves having trouble filming the scene, as it was nearly impossible to believe the moments that were unfolding before us. A wild ocelot was literally crawling on top of my head!

Mark made
mention of the
ocelot's size and
the fact it was
simply a kitten.
In all reality, this
animal was only
a few months old,
yet its growing
features, like a long
solid tail and large paws,
indicated that this animal would be
considered an adult very soon. At that
time, the cat would weigh closer to 40
pounds, making it a lethal shadow zone
predator searching for any unsuspecting
jungle prey.

Without warning, the cat leapt from atop my head and bounded off into the darkness. For a moment, we lost track of it in the underbrush, yet we weren't worried about the animal's return. This was a part of the game. Disappear, return, and pounce! I heard the rustling of leaves behind me, and without turning back to look, gazed toward the camera and asked if anyone could see the impending stalker.

With my arms in motion, I said, "Is it behind me right now? I feel like when I make sudden movements with my hands is when the ocelot pounces, and that's what they do. They creep up really slowly staying hidden within the shadows, and when they see a sudden movement..." I began to shake my left hand, and sure enough, as if on cue the cat sprang out of the darkness and latched onto my shoulder and neck.

"That's what they do right there... go right for the neck or the head in this case, ahhhh, jeez, I just got bit in the eye, and then... they have their dinner!"

The ocelot was in full 'play attack mode' and batted at my face with its paws. I was under siege, and the crew was laughing out loud at the sight of this epic onslaught of paws and bites.

"Ohhh, it's licking my ear... That's weird, I've never had my ear licked by an ocelot... but there's a first time for everything! Oh, now it's going for the back of my neck, this is good, the cat is practicing its hunting and this is exactly what they would do in the wild, go for the neck and bite down. But hopefully she's not going to inflict a death wound – ow, ow, ow!"

The cat was simply playing, but its teeth were also needle sharp, and with each little playful bite my neck was getting punched full of small holes!

I tried my best to continue narrating the encounter.

"Now, if I was one of this cat's littermates this is exactly how we would be playing, all teeth and claws. Trust me when I say those claws are sharp, those teeth are sharp... and I am getting little puncture marks, but it's nothing I can't take, not to be this close to such a cool rainforest creature!"

With the ocelot once again physically sitting on top of my head, I knew the moment was picture-perfect to give a signature close to the encounter. So, with a beaming smile on my face, I belted out to the camera, "I'm Coyote Peterson, Be Brave, Stay Wild... We'll see you on the next adventure!"

With a rolling tumble, the playful cat spilled off my hat and into my lap, rolled into the leaves, and sprang to its feet, following me as I walked off camera.

Mark called "CUT!" and then we regrouped as a team. We had some incredible moments of human/ocelot interaction captured on camera, but we needed more footage of just the cat. So, we took me out of the scene and spent time following the ocelot around in its natural environment.

From a respectful distance we watched in awe as this agile hunter put on a completely natural display of its abilities. The ocelot began climbing trees with ease, leaping from log to log and darting through a dense underbrush of vine tangles and palm fronds. This rainforest was truly the animal's playground, and as a camera team we were witness to something very few wildlife filmmakers have ever had the chance to document.

An animal enthusiast could go their entire life searching Central America, hoping to come across an ocelot, and never even catch a glimpse. These moments were truly priceless, and to this day, they are some of my fondest memories.

If the encounter could have lasted forever, I would have wished it so. However, all good things must come to an end. A sound off in the darkness caught the cat's attention, and we watched as it leapt down from its perch and darted off into the underbrush. We all held our breath, eyes fixed on the shadows that faded from the edges of our light beams, and waited. My eyes were wide with anticipation for the playful creature to return with a bounding leap into my arms; yet to my disappointment, nothing.

Still we waited until nearly 15 minutes had passed. I jingled my snake tongs, I rustled my adventure pack zippers and clasps... but the ocelot was gone.

Mark turned to me and said, "Did that really just happen? Dude... you might be the first animal show host to ever make contact with a wild ocelot, that was amazing!"

With flashlights guiding the way, we took our first steps back, starting the long hike that would lead to our jungle huts. We were alive with chatter, recounting the funniest moments of the soon to be famous ocelot encounter.

I am sure it's probably hard to believe the story you just read – Coyote Peterson palling around with a wild ocelot – but believe it or not, it's completely true. This kind of interaction with a wild animal is something that most people can only dream about. I was simply lucky enough to have lived it. As a wildlife enthusiast and a person who seeks adventure, I feel incredibly fortunate to have shared these moments with one truly special cat.

I am often asked what my *most* memorable animal encounter has been, and if you have gotten to this point in the book, now you know. It truly was the time I spent getting face to face with the incredible shadow stalker!

Conclusion

Looking back on the chapters you just read, I hope you felt a wave of emotion for the moments we shared on these epic adventures.

Having the opportunity to chronicle my bravest adventures into these pages really gave me the chance to expand upon the poetic nature I feel in my heart every time I break trail into the wild and get up close with animals. I did my best to lace thematic and inspirational elements into each chapter that hopefully allowed you to look at nature and its animals in a new light.

Where certain creatures like spiders and snakes may have once caused you fear, perhaps now you will look at them and think, they should not be feared, but rather admired. There were animals in this book that we very rarely see, like the snapping turtle or the ocelot, and perhaps now you will visit a library or spend time searching the Internet to learn more about these elusive predators. The environments we explored, from Alaska to Costa Rica, are some of the most beautiful and biologically diverse ecosystems in North America. Perhaps reading about them on the pages of this book has inspired you to muster up an unknown bravery you never knew you had, and in turn, has given you the confidence to go out and have an adventure of your own.

It seems we have reached the end of our adventure, but don't worry... I have a good feeling that if you liked this book, our journeys have only just begun.

Thank you for reading and for being a brave member of the Coyote Pack.

It's a wild world out there, and it's filled with wild animals, which means that my next series of Brave Adventures is soon to come.

I'm Coyote Peterson, Be Brave, Stay Wild... We'll see you on the next adventure!

Acknowledgements

To date there have been over 250 unique episodes on the Brave Wilderness Channel, and to take an adventure captured on camera and turn it into a story composed of words and illustrations was a feat far easier said than done. It was difficult to select only a handful of our animal encounters to be incorporated into the pages of this book, yet I think we did a fantastic job of leading the reader on one wild adventure.

Writing a book has been one of the most rewarding accomplishments in my 35 years of existence, and I couldn't have done it alone.

I would like to thank my business partner and fellow visionary Mark Laivins for his keen eye and attention to detail, producer Chance Ross for his ability to edit these stories and guide them to the finish line, longtime friend and illustrator Patrick Brickman for his incredible vision and artistic brilliance he lent to the book's cover illustration, animal enthusiast and illustrator Dia Windhoffer for her ability to really capture the vintage feel of a field guide journal, and Margret M. Krister (my Mom) for her breathtaking illustrations that perfectly captured the many priceless moments we all experienced through these adventures.

I would also like to thank Mango Publishing for their belief in this vision and for allowing us to run with our imaginations without restraint – they could not have been a better publishing partner – and Creative Artist Agency for helping us get these stories out to the world and for their support in continuing the growth of the Brave Wilderness brand.

And last but not least, to Chris Kost, who drew this amazing great horned owl!

See buddy, I told you that this picture would make the book!

Author Bio

Coyote Peterson, host of the *Brave Wilderness Network's* animal adventure shows, is first and foremost an avid explorer and animal enthusiast!

Since his very earliest memories as a child, animals have played a huge role in his life. Growing up in a rural suburb east of Cleveland, Ohio, Coyote spent most of his childhood outdoors scouring the nearby forests, swamps, and creek beds looking for whatever creatures he could get his hands on. From bullfrogs and water snakes, to his fascination with the common snapping turtle, each-and-every day was an adventure into the wild where there was always something new to encounter.

As Coyote passed through high school and into college, he found another passion in his love for movies, which led him to studying video production and directing at The Ohio State University. There, he honed his skills for telling stories, both behind and in front of the camera, before setting out to make narrative storytelling his career.

Coyote's intense passion for wildlife and video production inspired him to combine the two mediums. With entertainment as the catalyst, his goal was to make animal conservation and education entertaining for the next wave of outdoor explorers and animal enthusiasts.

To accomplish this feat, he and business partner Mark Laivins designed the Brave Wilderness brand, through which they produce several shows including *Breaking Trail*, *Beyond the Tide*, *Dragon Tails*, *Coyote's Backyard* and *On Location*. Each of these adventure series brings the audience up close with a plethora of animals in various locations, all while promoting **education** and conservation through exciting expeditions into the wild.

Coyote's vision for the future of the Brave Wilderness brand is vast, and whether he is diving into the water to catch a giant turtle, or putting himself up against the sting of a bullet ant, he aspires to educate and entertain above anything else.

Thank you for reading.

In writing Coyote Peterson's Brave Adventures, Coyote Peterson did his very best to produce the most accurate, well-written and mistake-free book. Yet, as with all things human (and certainly with books), mistakes are inevitable. Despite Coyote's and the publisher's best efforts at proofreading and editing, some number of errors will emerge as the book is read by more and more people.

We ask for your help in producing a more perfect book by sending us any errors you discover at **errata@mango.bz**. We will strive to correct these errors in future editions of this book. Thank you in advance for your help.